"Darcy has this crazy idea," Jake said.

At some point he had followed her into the kitchen and was leaning against the wall. Mariabella froze at the words. Darcy. That woman who had almost recognized her. Did she know? Had she figured it out after Mariabella left the restaurant?

Impossible. Wasn't it?

"Oh…yeah?" She fiddled with the flowers.

"She thinks you might be a princess."

Mariabella swallowed hard. She plucked out a daisy from the center and shoved it into a space on the side, then moved a rose from the right to the left. "Huh? Really?"

"Are you?"

The two words hung in her kitchen—heavy, fat with anticipation. Destructive.

Are you her?

It was over. Her life here. Her fantasy that she could be loved by a man like him as an ordinary woman. Once she told him who she was he would never look at her the same way again.

Dear Reader,

If you're reading this, chances are I've already got the lights and tree out at my house—and if they're not up, they will be soon. I have a hard time waiting until after Thanksgiving before I start Christmas preparations. I'm worse than a little kid! That's what makes writing these Christmas books so much fun for me. Every minute I spend in my characters' Christmas world gives me another dose of the holiday, complete with the decorations, the food and the warm memories.

Someone asked me once in an interview to name my favorite element of Christmas. For me, it's the music of the holiday. I start playing those songs as soon as they come on the radio, and don't turn them off until the day after Christmas. Every time I listen to a song like "Frosty the Snowman" I remember watching the Claymation movie with my kids (truth be told, they still haven't outgrown that movie classic). Singing along with "Hark the Herald Angels Sing" or "Silent Night" reminds me what the holiday is truly about and keeps me grounded in all the shopping madness.

I hope you have a wonderful holiday season, and a memorable Christmas this year. Please visit my Web site at www.shirleyjump.com, my blog at www.shirleyjump.blogspot.com or write to me at P.O. Box 5126, Fort Wayne, IN 46895. Merry Christmas—and may your stocking be filled with lots of books!

Best wishes,

Shirley

SHIRLEY JUMP

A Princess for Christmas

HARLEQUIN®

TORONTO • NEW YORK • LONDON
AMSTERDAM • PARIS • SYDNEY • HAMBURG
STOCKHOLM • ATHENS • TOKYO • MILAN • MADRID
PRAGUE • WARSAW • BUDAPEST • AUCKLAND

First, to my readers—
there is no more special gift than your letters, support and
warm words. You make writing an extra wonderful joy.

Second, to my family—
every day with you is a treasured present.

Recycling programs
for this product may
not exist in your area.

ISBN-13: 978-0-373-17617-5

A PRINCESS FOR CHRISTMAS

First North American Publication 2009.

Copyright © 2009 by Shirley Kawa-Jump, LLC.

New York Times bestselling author **Shirley Jump** didn't have the willpower to diet, nor the talent to master under-eye concealer, so she bowed out of a career in television and opted instead for a career where she could be paid to eat at her desk—writing. At first, seeking revenge on her children for their grocery-store tantrums, she sold embarrassing essays about them to anthologies. However, it wasn't enough to feed her growing addiction to writing. So she turned to the world of romance novels, where messes are (usually) cleaned up before The End. In the worlds Shirley gets to create and control, the children listen to their parents, the husbands always remember holidays and the housework is magically done by elves. Though she's thrilled to see her books in stores around the world, Shirley mostly writes because it gives her an excuse to avoid cleaning the toilets and helps feed her shoe habit. To learn more, visit her Web site at www.shirleyjump.com.

Praise for Shirley Jump:

"Shirley Jump's *Miracle on Christmas Eve* has a solid plot and [an] involving conflict, and the characters are wonderful."
—*Romantic Times BOOKreviews*

About *Sweetheart Lost and Found*
"This tale of rekindled love is right on target;
a delightful start to this uplifting, marriage-oriented series
[THE WEDDING PLANNERS]."
—*LibraryJournal.com*

About *New York Times* bestselling anthology *Sugar and Spice*
"Jump's office romance gives the collection a kick,
with fiery writing."
—*PublishersWeekly.com*

This season Harlequin® Romance brings you

Christmas Treats

For an extra-special treat this Christmas
don't look under the Christmas tree or in
your stocking—pick up one of your favorite
Harlequin Romance novels, curl up and relax!

From presents to proposals, mistletoe to marriage,
we promise to deliver seasonal warmth, wonder
and, of course, the unbeatable rush of romance!

*And look out for Christmas extras in all of your
November Harlequin Romance titles!*

CHAPTER ONE

THE woman in the painting whispered to Mariabella. Her deep green eyes, slightly hooded by heavy lashes, seemed to hold a quiet secret. One she kept close to her heart, one perhaps she hadn't even shared with the man who'd held the paintbrush.

Mariabella reached out, traced the air around the painted woman's eyes. Secrets. This woman had one.

And so, too, did Mariabella Romano.

"You like that painting, huh?"

Mariabella started, jerked out of her reverie. She turned at the sound of Carmen's voice. More friend than employee, Carmen Edelman had worked for Mariabella ever since she'd opened the Harborside Art Gallery in the little coastal Massachusetts town almost a year ago. The quirky college graduate had walked in one day, her arms loaded with paintings, each one a gem. Ever since, Carmen had been unearthing wonderful finds, including the artist who'd painted the portrait of the mysterious woman, titled simply, *She Who Knows.*

Mariabella's twenty-five-year-old assistant had an uncanny eye for quality work, and had been instrumental in helping Mariabella choose the paintings for the gallery's upcoming Christmas show. Carmen's bohemian personality gave the gallery—and Mariabella—a little something unexpected every day.

"I do love this piece," Mariabella said, pointing toward the portrait of the brunette. "It has a certain depth and mystery to it. It is my favorite piece in the collection."

"It does seem to have good karma, doesn't it?" Carmen took a step back, propped a fist beneath her chin, sending dozens of silver and gold bracelets on a jingling race down her arm. "Such deep thoughts in each brush stroke. What do you think it's saying?"

"Probably what she knows...and no one else does."

Carmen turned and caught Mariabella's eye. Her black pageboy haircut swung forward with the movement, and her red-rimmed cat's-eye glasses slipped a little on her nose. "Oh, so perceptive! I can see that now. The way the woman has her chin tilted down just a bit, the way her hair is brushed across her eyes, like she wants to hide behind the bangs but can't because they're not quite long enough. Hmm...though that could just be a bad haircut. And then there's the way her hand is coming up to cover her mouth. It's like she has..."

"Secrets," Mariabella finished, then wanted to catch the word and bring it back. But really, Carmen—like everyone else in town—didn't know anything about the true identity of Mariabella "Romano."

Who wasn't a Romano at all.

Money and privilege provided the opportunity to buy anything—including a new identity and a temporary escape from a life that had chafed at Mariabella like a too-tight yoke.

Carmen's scarlet lips spread in a wide smile. "This is why I love working for you. You're, like, totally psychic about art. You have such a gift."

The genuine compliment washed over Mariabella. She'd lived her life surrounded by people who had dropped compliments on her like confetti at a parade—with the words having about as much depth and meaning. She'd found herself feeling as vacant as those words, and needing something...more.

So a little more than a year ago, she'd left that insular, empty world behind, shedding her true name and her heritage to come here, searching for—

Reality. Peace. Independence.

Here, in Carmen's words, her gaze, and also in the friends who filled the shops lining Harborside's boardwalk, Mariabella had exactly that. People who saw her, not for her lineage, but for herself.

"Speaking of gifts, when are you going to share *your* gifts with the world?" Carmen drifted over to the store's Christmas tree and hoisted one of the faux presents that sat below the tabletop display. "And I'm not talking about these empty boxes."

Sometimes—like when they were dealing with a difficult artist—Mariabella considered her employee's persistence a blessing. And other times when she called it more of a curse.

Like now.

"A gallery is not meant to be used as the owner's ego trip."

"Mar, you're not even on the baggage carousel."

"Baggage…what?"

Carmen waved a hand. "American translation, you're not taking any risks. At all. And for your information, it's not a big deal to hang a few of your pieces here. People want to get a peek into who you are, and what's going on in your noggin." Carmen tapped her head.

"Carmen, we go through this argument every week—"

"For good reason—"

"And the answer is always the same."

"Doesn't make it the right answer." Carmen arched a thinly penciled brow.

"My paintings are hardly ready." The lie slipped easily from Mariabella's tongue. She'd been to art school, received her master's degree. She knew when a painting had fulfilled its potential on the canvas. Even though she wouldn't call her art ready for the Louvre, by any stretch, the pieces she'd created could hang proudly on these walls.

If she dared to put her soul on display.

There was something inherently intimate about hanging art on a gallery wall, something that allowed, as Carmen had said, the world a peek inside the artist's true self. And Mariabella knew that as long as she was living a lie, she couldn't permit even a single glimpse.

"In addition," Mariabella went on, when she saw Carmen readying another objection, "we have a number of artists scheduled to exhibit, enough to carry us through next year. Our walls are full, Carmen." Mariabella returned to the front desk of the gallery, and started reviewing the proofs of the catalog for next Tuesday's show. The holiday tourist season was in full swing, and as the calendar flipped closer to Christmas, more and more people flocked to the seaside community looking for unique, locally made gifts. Harborside decorated its boardwalk, revved up its restaurants, brewed up special seasonal lattes, and after a post-summer slumber, came back to life in a new and festive way.

It hadn't been that way in years' past. Before Mariabella came to town, Harborside used to lock its shutters and close its doors for the winter, all the residents and business owners hibernating like bears. Mariabella had joined the Community Development Committee, seeing a potential for more in the little town. That enthusiasm had gotten her elected to committee chair, and also spurred the town into action. This year would be the second that Harborside used the holiday season to bring in much-needed winter revenue through a series of events. The boost in tourism dollars—albeit not a large amount yet, but one that was growing—seemed to have everyone humming Christmas carols.

Carmen's hand blocked Mariabella's view. The bangle bracelets reprised their jingle song. "An excuse is still an excuse, even if you wrap it up with a pretty bow. Or in your case, a European accent."

Mariabella laughed. "Are you ever going to give up?"

"Not until I see a Mariabella masterpiece—" Carmen framed her fingers together and squinted through the square at the wall "—right there. That space would be perfectamundo."

"Uh-huh. And getting this catalog to the printer's before the end of the day would also be…" Mariabella paused. "How do you say?"

"Perfectamundo." Carmen grinned.

"*Perfectamunda,* yes?"

"Close enough. Eventually I'll have you talking all slang, all the time."

Mariabella shook her head and got back to work. Slang—coming from her cultured tongue. She could just imagine her father's reaction to *that.* His stony face, rigid posture. But worst of all, the silence. She'd hated the judgment in that quiet.

She'd never measured up, not to his standards, voiced or not. She'd never sat still enough, smiled at enough people, acted as he'd expected.

Acted as a *princess* should.

If he could see her now, her hair loose and flowing, dressed in jeans and spiky heels, paint beneath her fingernails from a frenzied creative streak this morning—

Well, he couldn't see her, and that was the best part about Harborside being located on the other side of the world. That freedom, to be herself, was a large part of what Mariabella loved about being here. And even talking slang. She smiled to herself.

"Hey." Carmen nudged Mariabella. "Did you see that?"

"What?"

"Eye candy, two o'clock."

"Eye…what?"

"Cute guy, walking past the gallery." She nudged Mariabella's shoulder a second time.

"Mmm…okay." Mariabella kept working on the catalog's corrections.

Carmen let out a frustrated gust. "You should go talk to him."

That got Mariabella's attention. "Go talk to him? Why?"

"Because he's alone, and you're alone, and it's about time you took number one, a few hours for yourself, and number two, a step out of that comfort zone you're so determined to stay glued to."

Mariabella wanted to tell Carmen she had already taken a giant step out of her comfort zone, something beyond opening the gallery. A step that had brought her all the way across the world, from a tiny little country outside of Italy to here, an even tinier town in Massachusetts.

To a new life. A life without kings and queens.

Without expectations.

Carmen did have a point about the dating, though. In all the time Mariabella had been in Harborside, she hadn't dated anyone, hadn't gotten close to a man. She'd made friends, yes, but not true relationships, nothing deep. Part of that was because she'd had no time, as Carmen mentioned, but a bigger part was self-preservation.

She thought again of the woman in the painting. Had that woman dared to open her heart?

If so, was the price she'd had to pay as high as Mariabella's?

"Let's focus on catalogs and canapés, instead of my love life," Mariabella said to her assistant. "I think the artist will be upset if I tell him I spent my time pursuing a hot date instead of concentrating on his show."

Carmen turned to Mariabella and opened her mouth, as if she wanted to argue the point, then shut it again. "Okay. I can see when the stars are out of alignment for this topic. I'll zip down to Make it Memorable and check on the appetizers for Tuesday's opening."

Mariabella sent up a wave, while she kept on checking the page proofs. "Thank you. I'll hold down the tent."

Carmen laughed. "Fort, Mariabella. Fort."

Heat filled Mariabella's cheeks. Her accented English was flawless, but she'd yet to master all those odd little idioms. "I meant fort."

"Hey, a horse is still a horse, even if you call it a pony." Carmen toodled a wave, then left the gallery, with the hurried step that marked her every movement.

Soft, jazzy Christmas music flowing from the gallery's sound system provided companion noise for Mariabella as she got back to work. She settled onto a chair behind the counter, content to be alone, surrounded by the art she loved. All her life, she'd craved this kind of shop, this exact kind of cozy gallery. There were many days when she couldn't believe she actually owned this place, and had seen this dream come true. It made up for all those arguments with her father, all the tears she'd shed.

She paused a moment and cast a glance out the bay window behind her, drawing in the view of the ocean that lay down the dock from the gallery. Through the window, the sun-drenched day could have passed for summer, if the calendar didn't read a few days before Christmas. No snow lay on the ground yet, though the temperature outside was all winter. The ocean curled gently in and out, while seagulls dipped down to the beach for a late morning meal. Bright sunshine cast sparkles of light over the water. How different Harborside was from where Mariabella had grown up, yet how similar, too. She'd lived on the coast then, too, but that coast had been full of rocky cliffs, houses nestled among the stone paths and lush landscape. Here, the land was less hilly, more populated and didn't have hundreds of years of history carved into the side of every building. But Harborside offered something else Mariabella couldn't have in her old home. Something precious.

Anonymity.

A sense of peace draped over Mariabella like a cozy blanket. She loved this town, loved the haven she had found here. She thought of the letter in her purse, and wondered what answer she could possibly give. How she could ever explain she had found something in Harborside that she could never imagine leaving.

But soon, duty demanded her return. As always.

The bell over the door jingled and Mariabella jerked to attention. The man she and Carmen had seen earlier stood in the doorway, his tall figure cutting an imposing stance.

"May I help you?" Mariabella said, moving away from the front desk.

"Just looking, thank you." He stepped inside, giving Mariabella a better view of him.

Dark hair, dark eyes. What appeared to be an athletic build beneath the navy pinstriped suit, clearly tailored to fit his frame. She recognized his shoes as designer, his briefcase as fine leather. No ordinary tourist, that was clear. Most people who came to Harborside wore jeans in winter or shorts in the summer—dressed to relax and make the most of the boating, swimming and fishing the coastal town had to offer.

This man looked ready to steer a corporation, not a catamaran.

He stood about six feet tall, maybe six-two, and when he moved about the open space of the gallery, he had the stride of a man who knew his place in the world.

A zing of attraction ran through Mariabella. No wonder Carmen had called him eye candy. He had more to offer than a ten-pound chocolate bar.

"Our main gallery houses the artist in residence," she said, falling into step a few feet away from him, "who has some mixed media pieces in his collection as well as a number of portraits. In the west room, you will find our sculptures and art deco pieces, and the east room, which overlooks the ocean, features our landscapes, if you're looking for a picture of Harborside to take home or back to your office."

"I'm not looking for something for my home. Or office."

He barely glanced at her as he said the words, but more, he hadn't looked at a single painting. His gaze went, not to the landscapes, portraits and fresco panels, but to the—

Walls. The ceiling. The floors.

Then to her.

A chill chased up her spine.

Had they found her? Was her time here over? No, no, it couldn't be. She had two more months. That was the agreement.

It was too soon, she wasn't ready to leave. She loved her home, loved her gallery, and she didn't want to go back. Not yet.

Mariabella hung back, watching the stranger. He paused to look out the window, the one that provided a view of the entire boardwalk. He took a few steps, as if assessing all of Harborside, then returned to his perusal of the main room of Harborside Art Gallery.

Perhaps he hadn't come here after her. Perhaps he was only sizing up the gallery. Maybe he owned a place in a nearby town and he'd come here to check out the competition.

Except…

Doubt nagged at Mariabella. A whisper of more here, a hidden agenda. But what?

He entered the east room of the gallery, Mariabella's favorite space because of its location facing the harbor. Most of her sales, at least to outsiders, happened in that room. Tourists often selected a painting that captured a moment from their vacation, an image of a sunset, a burst of a sunrise over the ocean. Mariabella often commissioned works based solely on tourists' comments, filling the walls with works that held their visions and happy memories of Harborside.

But this man didn't stop to notice the view of the ocean

outside the window facing the Atlantic. He didn't glance at a single oil or watercolor. He merely strode the perimeter of the room, then exited, and headed into the third room. Again, not a flicker of his gaze toward the exquisite sculptures, nor a blink of the eye when he passed the multicolored art deco pieces.

His silence frayed at the edges of Mariabella's nerves. She paced the small area behind the front desk in the main gallery, unable to concentrate on the catalog. On anything but why he was here.

She needed to find a way to ask his intentions, without seeming to be asking. When he reentered the main room, she crossed to him. "May I offer you a cup of coffee? Tea?"

"Coffee. Black."

Again, barely a flicker of attention toward her. His mind seemed on something else. She let out a breath of relief as she crossed to the small table holding a carafe of fresh coffee, filled a cup, then loaded a small plate with raspberry thumb-print cookies. She turned—

And found him right behind her.

"Here is…here is your coffee. And these cookies—" Mariabella forced herself to breathe, not to betray the nervous-ness churning in her gut "—were baked by a local chef."

His attention perked at that. "Chef? Does he have a restau-rant?"

"She, and no, Savannah Dawson is the owner of Make it Memorable, the catering company in town."

He nodded, taking that in, but otherwise not responding to the information. Damn, he made her nervous. Nor did he accept a cookie. Instead, he merely sipped at the coffee, watching her. "And who are you?"

He didn't know her name. That meant he wasn't here for her.

Unless the question had been a ruse. No, she doubted that. He didn't look like a reporter, and didn't have the accent that said he'd been sent by her parents.

She'd worried for nothing. He was simply another tourist, albeit, not the most friendly one.

"Mariabella Romano," she said, putting out her hand, and with it, a smile, "gallery—"

"Thank you. That's all I needed." Then he turned and began to walk toward the door. That was it? No return of his name? No explanation why he had come here?

On any other day, she would have let this go. Not everyone who walked through the doors of Harborside Art Gallery walked back out with a piece of art. But this man—

This man had an agenda; she could feel it in her bones. And somewhere on his list, was her gallery.

A surge of fierce protectiveness rose in Mariabella's chest, overriding decorum and tact. "Who are you?"

He paused at the door, his hand on the brass handle, and turned back to face her. A shadow had dropped over his face, from the awning outside, but more, it seemed, from something inside him that he didn't want to tell her. "I'm…an investor."

"Well, sir, if you are thinking you are going to buy this shop, think again." She took a step closer to him, emphasizing her point. Like a terrier guarding her territory. "The owner loves this place. She will never sell."

A smile took over his face, but it held no trace of friendliness, not a hint of niceness. "Oh, I don't want this shop."

Relief flooded Mariabella. She'd read him wrong, he wanted nothing to do with her precious Harborside Art Gallery. Or her. Thank God. "Good."

That smile widened, and dread sunk in Mariabella's gut. And then she knew—she'd gotten it all wrong. She hadn't read him right at all.

"I want the entire block," he said. "By the end of the week would be convenient."

CHAPTER TWO

JAKE LATTIMORE peered down the boardwalk of Harborside, Massachusetts, and knew he didn't see the same thing the other people did. The brightly waving flags on the masts of the few covered boats wintered in the marina didn't beckon to him. The shop windows hawking T-shirts and sunglasses didn't attract his attention. The cafes and coffee shops, their doors swinging open and shut as people drifted in and out, sending tantalizing scented snippets of their menus into the air didn't call to his appetite.

No, what Jake saw wasn't even there. Yet.

Condos. A hotel. Maybe even an amusement park, and down the beach, Jet Ski rentals, parasailing stations.

By this summer, if at all possible, so profits could start rolling in immediately.

In other words, a vacation mecca, one that would expand his—and that of his financial backers—portfolio, and take this sleepy little town up several notches.

He glanced again at the boardwalk, at the festive holiday decorations. The notes of a Christmas song carried on the air as someone walked out of the stained-glass shop across the street. The melody struck a memory in Jake's heart, followed by a sharp pang.

A long time ago, this kind of place, this kind of setting,

would have had him rushing in to buy a gift. Humming along with the song. Thinking—

Well, he didn't think that anymore.

He got back to business. That was the only place heartache couldn't take root. Jake returned his attention to the facts and figures in his head, dismissing the sentimental images around him.

He'd done his research, ran his numbers, and knew without a doubt, Harborside was the perfect location for the next Lattimore Resort. Located along the Eastern seaboard, beneath Boston and above New York, away from the already congested areas of Cape Cod and Martha's Vineyard, the tiny town had been tucked away all this time, hardly noticed by tourists, just waiting for someone like him to come along and see its potential.

This was his specialty—find hidden treasures and turn them into profit machines.

This town would be no different. He'd find each shop owner's price, and pay it. Everyone, Jake had found, had a price.

He wouldn't let a little thing like dollars and cents get in the way of adding this resort to the Lattimore Properties empire. Not with so much on the line.

If he didn't land this deal, and went back to New York empty-handed, he knew what would happen. The whispers would start again. People saying he'd only been promoted to CEO because he was the Lattimore heir. Not because he had the chops to handle a project of this scope.

His father had handed him a challenge, sent him to prove he could achieve the goal on his own, and Jake had no intentions of doing anything but exactly that. He'd worked side by side with Lawrence Lattimore for five years, learning the business from the ground up. In the last year or two, though, his father had begun to lose his magic touch. Lawrence's decision making had become less sound, and the Lattimore Properties balance sheet showed the signs of his uneven hand.

The board began talking forced retirement, so his father had put Jake in charge and given him one directive:

Pull off a miracle.

When Jake returned to New York triumphant, with the Harborside jewel in his back pocket, no one could say the junior Lattimore wasn't up to the task of helming the multi-million dollar corporation. Lattimore Properties would once again be on the way to being the powerful company it had once been, and the downward slide that had begun under the last two years of Lawrence's tenure would be reversed.

"Who are you?"

He turned around and found the brunette from the art gallery standing behind him, fists propped on her hips, green eyes ablaze. She had a fiery demeanor about her, one that spoke of passion, in everything she did.

And that intrigued Jake. Very much.

"I told you. I'm an investor," he said. "In towns like this one."

Her lips pursed. "Let me save you some trouble. No one here is looking to sell their shops."

He arched a brow. "And you know this because…?"

"Because I live here. And I'm the chair of the Community Development Committee. It is my job to know."

He smirked. "And that makes you an expert on every resident?"

"It certainly gives me more insight than you."

He loved her accent. Lilting, lyrical. Even when she argued with him, it sounded like a song.

"You think so?" he said, taking a step closer to her. When he did, he caught a whiff of the floral notes of her perfume. Sweet, light. Tantalizing. "I've seen hundreds of towns like Harborside. And met dozens of people like you, people who have this romanticized vision of their town."

"How dare—"

"What they don't realize is that underneath all that coziness," he went on, "is a struggling seaport town that depends on one season of the year, maybe two, for all its financial needs. How much money do you think the people here make off the tourists who visit between the three months of summer and few weeks of Christmas? Enough to sustain every business and every resident for the other eight months of the year?"

She didn't answer.

"You and I both know it isn't." He gestured toward the town, from one end of the boardwalk to the other. This town—and this woman—didn't even realize what a boon a Lattimore resort would be. How it could bring *twelve* months of financial return. Every resident could benefit from a hotel like this, if they'd just imagine something different. "This place is quaint. Off the beaten path. And that's half the problem. Without something to draw visitors in, and really keep them here year-round, you might as well hang up the Going Out of Business signs now."

She glared at him. "We are doing fine."

He arched a brow. He'd read the statistics on Harborside. Talked to several of the business owners. He knew the tax base, the annual business revenue of each of the cottage industries lining the boardwalk.

They needed a bigger draw for tourists to sustain them—they knew it, he knew it. The only one not facing reality was Mariabella Romano.

"We do not need you," she insisted. "Or your coldhearted analysis of our town. Go find someplace else to expand your control of the world."

"Sorry. I'm here to stay."

The fist went back to her hip. She drew herself up, facing him down. Frustration colored her face. "Do not bother to unpack because you will not find anyone who will sell to you here. We all love Harborside just the way it is."

This woman didn't have any idea what she was up against.

This was going to be fun. A challenge. Something Jake hadn't had in a long time.

His pulse raced, and he found himself looking forward to the days ahead. To interacting with her especially. "I can be pretty persuasive, Miss Romano. We'll see how you feel about holding onto that little gallery after you hear my arguments for selling."

"And I can be terribly stubborn." She flashed him a smile of her own, one that held a hundred watts of power, but not a trace of neighborly greeting. "And you will never persuade me to sell so much as a coloring page to you."

Mariabella stood in her gallery and seethed. To think she'd found that man attractive!

No longer. He clearly had some kind of plans for Harborside and for that, she wouldn't give him so much as a single line in her social notebook. Christmas was only a few days away, surely the man would have somewhere to go—some fool who wanted to spend time with him over the holiday—and he could leave, taking his "investment" ideas with him.

Her cell phone rang, the vibrations sending the slim device dancing across the countertop. Mariabella grabbed the phone, just before it waltzed itself right off the edge. "Hello?"

"*Mia bella!* How are you?" her mother asked in their native language, one that was close to the Italian spoken in the country bordering their own country of Uccelli. Their small little monarchy, almost forgotten in Europe, had its own flavor, a mix of the heritages surrounding it.

"*Mama!*" Immediately, Mariabella also slipped into her home language, the musical syllables falling from her tongue with ease. Mariabella settled onto the seat behind her and held the phone close, wishing she could do the same with her mother. "I'm fine. And you? Papa?"

"Ah, we are about the same as always. Some of us are getting older and more stubborn."

Mariabella sighed. That meant nothing had changed at home. After all this time, Mariabella had hoped maybe her father had softened. Maybe he might begin to see his daughter's need for independence, for a life away from the castle.

He never had. He'd predestined his firstborn's path from the moment she'd been conceived, and never considered another option.

"But…" Her mother paused. "Your father is…"

The hesitation caused an alarm to ring in Mariabella's heart. Her mother, a strong, tall, confident woman never hesitated. Never paused a moment for anything. She had sat steadfast by her husband's side for forty years as he led Uccelli, weathering the roller coaster of changes that came with a monarchy. She'd done it without complaint. Without a moment of wavering from her commitment.

"Papa is what?"

"Having a little heart trouble. Nothing to worry about. We have the best doctors here, *cara*. You know that."

The letter in her back pocket seemed to weigh ten times more than it had this morning. Her father's demand that she return home immediately and take her rightful place in the family. She'd brushed it off when it had arrived, but maybe he'd sent the missive because his illness was worse than her mother was saying. Mariabella sent up a silent prayer for her father's health. He'd always been so hearty, so indestructible. And now—

"Is he going to be all right?"

"He'll be fine. Allegra has been wonderful about stepping in for him."

Her middle sister. The one who had always enjoyed palace life. Of the three Santaro girls, Allegra was the one who loved the state dinners, the conversations with dignitaries, the museum openings and policy discussions. She had sat by their father's side for more state business than any of the Santaro women—and for naught, because as the second-born, she was not first in line for the throne.

"I'm glad she's there," Mariabella said.

"I am, too. Your father misses you, of course, but he is happy to have Allegra with him. For now." Unspoken words hung in her mother's sentence.

Mariabella's father had made it clear he expected his eldest to return and take her place as the heir to the throne. Allegra was merely a placeholder.

Her father had voiced his displeasure several times about Mariabella's choice to leave the castle and pursue her dream of painting. At first, he'd talked of disowning her, until her mother had intervened. He'd relented, and given her a deadline. She'd been given a little over a year and a half—the time between college graduation and her twenty-fifth birthday, in February—and then she had to return.

Or—

Abdicate the crown and give up her family forever.

That was what her father had written. Choose the throne or be disowned. Mariabella hadn't told her mother, and suspected neither had her father.

"Don't worry," her mother said. "It will all be fine."

Easier said than done. She thought of her mother, and how worried Bianca Santaro must be about her husband. The miles between mother and daughter seemed to multiply. "I should come home. Be there for Christmas."

"I wish you could, *cara*. I would like nothing more than to have my daughter with me for Christmas." Her mother sighed, and Mariabella swore she could hear her mother begin to cry.

Half a world away, Mariabella's heart broke, too. Christmas. Her favorite holiday, and Mama's, too. The castle would already be decorated top to bottom with pine garlands and red bows. Christmas trees in every bedroom, set before every fireplace. None of them would top the giant tree, though, the twenty-five-foot beauty the palace's landscaper searched far and wide to find, then set in the center hall.

Every year, her mother personally oversaw the decorating of that tree, draping it in gold ribbons and white angel ornaments. And every year, it had been Mariabella's job to hang the last ornament on that tree. To be the one to pronounce it finished, and then to turn on the lights, washing the entire hall in a soft golden glow, sending a chorus of appreciation through the audience of onlookers brought in from the city.

But not this year. Or last year.

No, she had been here, instead. Leaving her mother to handle Christmas with her sisters. Who had lit the tree? Who had hung that last decoration?

"We will miss you," her mother said softly, "but if you come back, you know what will happen."

Mariabella let out a sigh. "Yes."

She would be expected to step back into her role. To go back to being groomed and primped for a crown she neither wanted nor asked to be given.

Because her father would not be convinced to let her go a second time. She knew that, as well as she knew her own name.

"Stay where you are," her mother said, as if reading her daughter's mind. "I know what this time, as limited as it is, means to you." Her mother's gentle orders were firm.

"Mama—"

"Don't argue with me, Bella. I sent you there. I know your father isn't happy, but I will deal with him. You deserve a life outside of this…birdcage."

That was, indeed, how Mariabella had come to think of life back home. A cage, a gilded one she could look out of, but not escape. People could stare inside, see her and judge her, but never really know her.

Then she'd come to Harborside and felt free, like a real person for the first time in her life.

"I'll call you if anything changes," her mother said, "but I have to say goodbye now. I'm late for a state dinner." She sighed. "You know how the prime minister gets. He hates to sit next to the visiting dignitaries from other countries and make small talk. The man has no social graces."

Mariabella laughed. She certainly didn't miss that part of palace life at all. The stuffy meals, the endless dinner parties. "Have a good time. If you can."

"Oh, I will. I seated the prime minister beside Carlita." Her mother let out a little giggle.

"Mama!"

"Your little sister will talk his ear off about horses and dressage. The man may just fall asleep before the soup arrives."

Mariabella laughed. Oh, how she missed some of those moments. The little fun they'd have behind the scenes, the laughter with her sisters, her mother. "I love you, Mama."

Her mother paused, and Mariabella could hear the catch in her voice when Bianca Santaro spoke again. "I love you too, *cara.*"

They ended the call, and Mariabella closed her phone, but held tight to the cell for a long time, as if she could hold her parents in the small electronic device. For a moment, she was back there, in her mother's bedroom, sitting on the chaise lounge, watching her mother get ready for a party. She saw Bianca brushing her hair, heard her humming a tune. Then she'd always turn and open her arms, welcoming her eldest daughter into her embrace. With Mama, there had always been time for a hug, a kiss, one more story before bed.

How she missed those days.

Even if she returned to Uccelli, those moments were gone forever. When her father stepped down, Mariabella was expected to fill the king's shoes. Which meant every day of her life in the palace had been spent grooming her for the throne.

If she returned, she'd be stepping right back into the middle of the very expectations she'd run from.

Her role as future queen.

Mariabella sighed. As much as she missed her parents and her homeland, she couldn't go back. Returning came at too steep a price.

Freedom.

Carmen came bursting through the door. Mariabella slipped her phone into her purse and with that movement, brought her mind back into work mode. She would dwell on the events across the world when she was alone.

"You will *never* believe what just happened when I was in Savannah's shop." Carmen slammed her hand on the counter in emphasis.

"An incredibly rude man offered to buy her place, yes?"

Carmen's jaw dropped. "How'd you know?"

"He was here, a few minutes ago. And wanted my gallery, too."

"The gallery, too?"

Mariabella nodded. "He wants the whole block. For some kind of 'investment.'" She put air quotes and a hint of sarcasm around the last word.

"In Harborside." Carmen said it as a statement, not a question. "That same cute guy we saw earlier."

Mariabella nodded again. "He is not so cute close-up, you know. Not when he is trying to turn our town into some kind of circus for tourists."

"Savannah tried to ask him questions, to find out what his plans are, but he didn't tell her more than boo." Carmen moved to the back of the counter and stuffed her purse underneath. "He's a big mystery man. I still think he's kind of cute, even if his plans might be diabolical. Or, maybe perfectly harmless. We'd have to find out more to know for sure."

"Well, cuteness will not win me over. Or convince me to sell."

Carmen shot her a grin. "You'd be surprised, Mariabella. Stronger women than you have been done in by blue eyes and a nice smile."

Mariabella glanced out the window again at the town she had come to love, to think of as her home. "Not me. And if this man thinks I will fall apart that easily, he can think again." She tucked a strand of hair behind her ear, then returned her attention to the catalog. "Because he has no idea who he is dealing with."

Truly, he had no idea. And neither did anyone in this town.

When the door of the limo shut, the sights and sounds of Harborside dropped away, leaving Jake alone with his thoughts.

Never a place he wanted to be.

He pulled out his PDA and started reading e-mails, at the same time powering up his laptop and scrolling through the reports he'd downloaded earlier about the town. The back of his limo had been his mobile office for as long as he could remember. The automobile had a satellite connection, to give him a link to the Web whenever he needed it, and a small desk installed between the seats for his laptop. Some days, it seemed as if he spent more time in this car than he did at home. If one could call his apartment in New York a home at all.

The passenger's side door opened and another man slid in. "Do you ever stop?"

Jake didn't look up. "I thought you went to lunch."

"I did. I'm done. Unlike you, I took a break from my job. I even made some friends."

Jake stopped working to stare at William Mason, his best friend and chauffeur, who had loosened his tie, and looked as relaxed as an out-of-town uncle at Thanksgiving dinner. Today, Will was sporting a red tie featuring reindeer leaping across the front, a glaring contrast to the white dress shirt with green pinstripes.

No one would call Will conventional. More than once, people had asked Jake why he didn't insist his chauffeur wear a more traditional dark suit and muted tie. Jake told them that if he wanted a conventional chauffeur, he would have hired one out of the phone book.

With Will, he'd gotten something no one else would have brought to the job—

Honesty. Loyalty. Friendship.

Three things Jake didn't seem to have in abundance, not in the vicious world of Lattimore Properties.

Will grinned at Jake, waiting for an answer. His sandy brown hair had been mussed by the wind, his cheeks reddened. He looked like he'd had...fun.

"How could you make friends?" Jake asked. "We've been in this town less than an hour."

"It doesn't take days to say, 'Hey, I'm Will, who are you?'"

"You didn't."

"I did." He shrugged. "Well, maybe something close to that. It would do you good to do the same."

Jake snorted. He could just see himself going into the local diner and introducing himself to a perfect stranger. Will had the affable personality to pull that off. He always had. Jake...well, Jake didn't. "Why would I? I'm here to complete a business deal, not win a popularity contest."

Will leaned forward, propping his elbows on his knees. "Have you ever found it odd that your best friend is a chauffeur? That you spend the last few days before Christmas working obsessively, instead of cuddling by a fire with some hot woman? Which is where I would be, I might add, at home, with my wife, if you weren't keeping me on the road, working more than Santa does. My wife, by the way, has learned to curse your name in three different languages because of the hours I work."

"I pay you well enough."

"Sometimes it's about time, not money, Jake." Will put his hands up before Jake could voice another objection. "I'm just saying, you might want to try the whole staying-home-with-a-girlfriend thing sometime."

"One—" Jake put out a finger "—my best friend is my chauffeur because you have been my best friend since we were kids, and I wanted to hire someone I trusted to drive me around. Especially since I'm going to spend half the day with you. Two—" he put out another finger "—I don't need more friends—"

"One friend is just so many you thought you might lose count after that?"

"And three—" Jake went on, putting out a third finger "—I'm not at home in front of a fire with a hot woman because I'm not dating anyone."

"Exactly the problem. You're going to be thirty this year, Jake. Don't you ever wonder what life would be like if you had one?"

"Had one what?"

"A life. Outside of that." Will waved at the PDA and laptop. "Inanimate objects aren't the most affectionate beings on the planet, in case you haven't noticed."

Jake scowled and ignored Will. He'd had what Will was talking about once before—had even expected by this age to be going home to a wife, just as his best friend did at the end of the day.

But fate had another future in mind. And Jake wasn't about to risk that kind of pain again. Once was enough.

"All I'm saying," Will persisted, "is that it's Christmas and it might be nice if you gave yourself a present this year."

"No one buys themselves gifts on Christmas. Or at least they're not supposed to."

"I meant a *present*. A life outside of work. Someone to wake up to." Will leaned forward and waited until Jake's gaze met his. "You had that once. And it sure would be nice to see you that happy again. Real nice." Will got out of the car and shut the door.

"That's where you're wrong," Jake muttered to the closed door. "That kind of happiness doesn't happen twice." And he went back to where he found peace.

In those inanimate objects that didn't leave him. And didn't die.

CHAPTER THREE

"He's back," Carmen said, tugging on Mariabella's sleeve.

Mariabella turned away from the customer she was talking to, and saw the stranger from earlier cross by her front windows. Not him again.

She'd hoped she'd made her feelings clear this morning. Between that, and Savannah's refusal to sell, the man should have let by now, realizing his "investments" weren't welcome in Harborside.

Apparently, he was a slow learner.

"Carmen, can you help this lady find a painting for over her sofa?" Mariabella said, gesturing to the middle-aged woman beside her, who had entered the gallery just a few minutes earlier. "She is looking for something with tones of rose and cream."

"Certainly. Right this way," Carmen said, pointing toward the second room of the gallery. "We have some singularly cool sunsets that I think will be perfect for what you want."

"Wonderful!" the customer exclaimed. "I have this huge blank wall in the great room just crying out for something spectacular."

Carmen grinned. "If you want spectacular, you've come to the right place."

The woman followed Carmen into the next room, the two

of them chatting about the exquisite sunsets each had seen in Harborside, while Mariabella headed out of the gallery and in the direction she'd seen the stranger go earlier.

She didn't see him. But she did see a long, black limousine parked across the street, in the public parking lot.

His, she was sure.

The driver sat behind the wheel, sedate and patient. Probably bored out of his mind, waiting on Mr. Investment to finish his fruitless quest for real estate.

"Mariabella!"

She turned at the sound of the familiar voice. "Miss Louisa. How are things with you?"

The older lady hurried over to Mariabella, her portly dachshund tottering at her feet, his four legs struggling to walk underneath the thick red Santa coat Louisa Brant had buckled around the long, short-haired dog. "Have you heard the latest? About that man trying to buy up our property?"

"I have. And I am not selling."

"I was thinking about it. You know how I hate the winters here. It sure would be nice to retire in Florida. Take me and my little George here down to a sunny little place for the rest of our days." She let out a long sigh, and clasped her thick wool coat tighter, as if just the thought had her feeling winter's chill a little more.

"If you do, who would head the women's tea every New Year?"

Louisa patted Mariabella's hand. "Now, dear, you know that's hardly my doing at all. You're the one who takes care of all of us in this town. Why you're practically a one-woman organizing dynamo. I don't know how little Harborside existed before you came along. You've got us holding dances, and teas, and summer regattas and all kinds of things. This place has become a regular hotbed of activity." Louisa laughed. "Or maybe a hot water bottle, considering how tiny we are."

Mariabella smiled. "I am not doing this alone. I have a lot of help."

"Every spear has a point, you know." Louisa's dog gave a tug on the leash, straining toward the park on the other side of the street. "Well, I must be going."

"Miss Louisa—"

The older woman turned back. "Yes, dear?"

"Promise me you'll talk to me before you consider selling to that man. We businesses in Harborside have to stick together. Surely, as a group, we'll be fine."

Louisa smiled, but her smile shook a little. "Of course, dear."

Then she was gone, the dachshund's tail wagging happily. He seemed to be the only one pleased with the way the conversation had ended.

Mariabella redoubled her determination to rid Harborside of this interloper. As long as he was here, people would continue to be upset and worried about their futures. Louisa loved her shop and had never mentioned retiring before today. Once this stranger was gone, everyone would calm down again and business would return to normal. She returned her attention to his limo, and to the license plate.

Okay, so now she knew two things. He was wealthy. And he was from out of town, but not so far that the distance couldn't be driven. She hurried down the sidewalk and peered around a telephone pole at the limo's license plates.

New York. She started memorizing the numbers, intending to call Reynaldo and have him—

"Checking me out?"

Mariabella jumped at the sound of his voice, and pivoted back. The man stood a mere two feet behind her, close enough that she could see the shades of cobalt flecked with gold in his eyes. See the sharp angle of his jaw, catch the woodsy scent of his cologne. Notice him three times more than she had earlier today.

But not be affected one iota. At all.

"Yes." Damn. She hated having to admit that to him. He'd startled her and she couldn't come up with another excuse.

"I'm no criminal, I assure you, and I have only the best intentions."

"Depends on who you ask, and how you interpret your intentions."

A smirk raised one side of his lips. "Touché."

She glanced back over her shoulder at the limo, trying again to memorize the numbers on the license plate. If this man wasn't going to tell her who he was or why he was here, she would find out for herself.

"Planning on playing detective?" he asked, reading her mind.

"No." Mariabella was not much better at lying than she was with idioms, and a flush filled her cheeks.

"I'll save you the trouble of bothering the local police chief. Not that he seems to have much to do in a town this size." The man reached into his suit jacket, withdrew a slim silver case and produced a business card. "Jacob Lattimore, CEO of Lattimore Properties."

She took the embossed white linen card. It was simple and clean, giving only a New York address and an office telephone number. Nothing that told her who he was, or why he had picked her town—and she *had* come to think of Harborside as hers, ever since the little community had welcomed her, without reservation—and what he intended to do here. "What kind of properties?"

"Resorts. Vacation properties. Condos, hotels."

Mariabella's jaw dropped. "Harborside is not that kind of town."

Another smile, the kind she was beginning to hate. "It can be, once the owners of the shops along this boardwalk see how a Lattimore resort can transform this place into a money machine for everyone." He waved a hand down the length of the boardwalk, as if he were a magician, making all of it disappear, and in its place, creating a gargantuan eyesore of a hotel.

Thus turning Harborside into a cartoon version of what it was right now, something he'd stamp on some silly brochure and market to travelers, as a "destination."

Panic gripped Mariabella. He couldn't be serious. If he did this, he would destroy the very refuge she had found. Ruin the small little town that had wrapped around her, safe and secure, like the cottage she'd been renting. Turning Harborside into a resort town would not only change the very fabric of the community, but worse, it would attract the very people she had tried so hard to avoid all these years—

Her peers. Her family. And worst of all, the media.

If any of the above came to Harborside, her biggest nightmare would come to life.

And her secrets would be exposed.

Her world here would be ripped apart, and she would be forced to return to the one she had left. Forced to step up and take her rightful place beside her mother and father. And eventually, *on* the throne.

No. She wasn't ready, not yet. She had more time, not much, but a little, and she needed it desperately to have this…

Normalcy. Peace. Anonymity.

And then, maybe, yes, she could go back to the birdcage. But on her terms, not Jacob Lattimore's.

She had to stop this man. Had to convince the other business owners on the Community Development Committee to hold firm, and refuse to sell. Surely, as a group, they would have the strength necessary to fend off his offers, no matter how tempting he made his financial proposals. Harborside would be preserved, just as it was, and Mariabella could be sure her town would never change.

"I understand you see this town as some kind of—" he waved vaguely "—step back in time. A little bit of nostalgia.

But nostalgia, unfortunately, doesn't always make money. You have to face reality, Miss Romano, you and the other business owners. Travelers want more on their vacations than a pretty view."

She stared at him and fumed. "There are some people who want a quiet place to stay, not a zoo."

"But not enough people. Your town is struggling, and the sooner you face the fact that you need a property like mine to shake things up, the better off everyone will be." He glanced around at the garland draped between the streetlights and the crimson bows hanging on the storefronts. "No amount of Christmas spirit—" the last two words slipped off his tongue with a taste of sarcasm "—will mask the scent of desperation."

"No one here is desperate."

He arched a brow. A silent disagreement.

Mariabella wanted to throw a thousand arguments in his face. Except, there were a few businesses along the boardwalk that had struggled in recent months, a fact she could not overlook, no matter how hard she tried. A few who would jump at the chance to retire, or find a buyer for buildings that housed inventory that hadn't sold in months. Harborside, like many seaside towns, struggled to compete for tourist dollars, and the members of the Community Development Committee had been brainstorming for months ways to increase traffic flow to the tiny town.

Jake Lattimore would not be the answer, no matter what. The town was not that desperate. To get rid of him, however, meant Mariabella needed to do whatever it took to protect what she loved.

Whatever it took.

Jake watched Mariabella Romano hurry down the sidewalk— in the opposite direction of her gallery—and had to admit he was intrigued.

She hated him.

And he liked that.

Clearly, he needed therapy, or a drink.

He opted for the drink. Faster, cheaper and easier. And in the opposite direction of the limo, where William had undoubtedly witnessed the entire exchange, and was waiting to offer his two cents about fireplaces and Christmas "presents."

Jake didn't need to hear that. Didn't need any more advice from well-meaning people who told him to move on with his life. He'd spent five years moving on—by working.

He gave Mariabella one last glance—she was beautiful, a tall woman with curves in all the right places—before ducking into the Clamshell Tavern. Blues music greeted him, along with a nautical décor. White painted pine walls, navy blue vinyl seats and life rings hanging on the walls printed with the restaurant's name.

All kitsch, all the time. Jake tried hard not to roll his eyes.

"Table for…one?" the hostess asked, peering around him, as if she thought he had a friend hiding in his pocket.

"I'll just sit at the bar. Thanks." He pushed through the glass doors and into the lounge area, which featured more of the same décor.

Good thing he rarely got seasick.

"What'll it be?" asked the bartender, a rotund man in a red-and-white striped shirt, something that was probably supposed to be pirate style, but came off looking more like barber shop clown.

"Your best vodka. Dry. Two olives."

The bartender nodded, then turned and mixed the drink. A minute later, he slid the glass in front of Jake and headed down to the opposite side of the bar.

An unappetizing mix of nuts and something resembling pretzels sat in a bowl to Jake's left. He pushed it away. What he wouldn't give for a tray with a good aged gouda, accompanied by a pear and cinnamon relish. Maybe a salad with grilled endive, apples and glazed fennel. Some *real* food, not this stuff that came out of a bag thrown together in a factory.

If he were back in New York, he'd have any gourmet food he wanted at his beck and call. He'd attended dinners, parties, openings, dining on the best the local chefs had to offer.

Lately, though, those platters had been leaving him with a feeling of emptiness, as if he could eat and eat and never have his fill. Or, as if every meal had too much fluff, and not enough substance.

Restlessness had invaded his sleep, his thought patterns— and at the worst possible time. He needed to be focused, aware, in order to execute this deal and prove himself to the company, while also boosting the bottom line.

Once the Harborside project was underway, surely that hole in his gut would fill.

It would.

"Well, you sure know how to rile people up around here, don't you?" A man slid onto the stool beside Jake. He had a shock of white hair, and wore a long flannel shirt over a pair of thick khakis. He looked about sixty-five, maybe seventy, and sat at the bar with the ease of someone who had been there a time or twenty. "The usual, Tony."

The bartender nodded, reached in the cooler and popped the top on a beer. He slid the dark beer down the bar to the older man, with a friendly hello, then went back to washing glasses.

"So, why are you doing it?" he said.

Jake pivoted toward the other man. "Are you talking to me?"

"Do you see someone else in this bar who's got the whole town in a tizzy?" The older man arched a brow, then put out his hand. "Name's Zeke Carson, short for Ezekiel, though no one calls me that and gets an answer. I'm the newspaper editor for this town, except our paper's more like a newsletter." He chuckled. "Small-town living. You gotta love it."

Jake shook with Zeke. Will would have been proud to see Jake making a friend, of sorts. An acquaintance, really, but at least he could go back to the limo and reassure Will he hadn't remained a hermit.

"Jake Lattimore." No sense keeping his name a secret any longer. Mariabella Romano had undoubtedly set Zeke on him, another guard dog to chase him out of town. If she hadn't already nailed up WANTED: DEAD OR ALIVE posters around town with his name and face on them, Jake figured it was only a matter of time.

Instead of annoying him, as something like that might on any other day, with any other project, it had him even more intrigued.

Charged up. Ready to rise to whatever challenge Mariabella threw his way.

He hadn't felt that way in a while. It had to be the Harborside project, not the woman, that had him feeling so challenged—because that was where his energies lay right now, and where they should lay.

Despite what Will had said, Jake had no intentions of entangling himself in another relationship. Especially not at this time of year.

He stared down into his drink, the frosted clear liquid a mirror to his heart. Five years ago this month.

Five years. Some days, it felt like five minutes.

Zeke took a sip of his beer. "I know who you are. Knew before you got here."

Jake arched a brow, pushing the other thoughts aside. "You did?"

"I may edit a small-town paper, Mr. Lattimore, but that doesn't make me stupid. I read the financial pages. I know all about your company, and I knew you were looking for some coastal properties to add to your portfolio." Zeke grinned. "Read it in an issue last month."

Jake nodded. "I'm impressed."

Zeke tipped his beer in Jake's direction. "I am, too. You're one of those wunderkinds. Rocketship to the top and all that."

Jake shrugged. He hated that label. Maybe he should color his hair gray. That might stop people from commenting on his status at the top of the company before he'd celebrated his thirtieth birthday.

"Must make your dad proud."

"Something like that," Jake said. He tugged his PDA out of his jacket pocket and began thumbing through his e-mails, hoping Zeke would get the hint and stop talking.

He didn't.

"'Cept your dad's had some troubles lately, I read. Company's struggling a little."

"It's fine," Jake said.

"And you…wasn't there something that happened a few years back…?" Zeke rubbed at his chin. "Can't remember what it was. Some accident and—"

"I'm not here to discuss my personal life, Mr. Carson." The words clipped off Jake's tongue. Harsher than he'd intended.

"Zeke, please."

"Zeke."

The other man didn't say anything for a minute. Jake hoped he'd given up on the conversation. Zeke drank his beer, watched the game on television. Then he shifted in his seat toward Jake again. "So, why Harborside?"

Jake thought of cutting off the conversation, then reconsidered. Perhaps talking to the local newspaper editor would be a good idea. Could garner some good press for Lattimore Properties. "You read the financial pages. You tell me, Zeke."

Zeke thought a second, clearly pleased to have his own brain picked. "It's undiscovered. Centrally located. Has just enough beach for one of your fancy-shmancy hotels, but not so much sand that the place'll get crowded with big bucks homeowners and their McMansions."

"So far, so good." Jake pushed the PDA aside, and reached for his drink, but didn't sip it.

"Let's see…" Zeke leaned forward, his gaze meeting Jake's. "You like a challenge, and Harborside is one. We're New Englanders. Stubborn, set in our ways. Not much for change of any kind. Hence, the big challenge. Why pick an unpopulated area, with no one to push around and bully when you corporate giants can go after this place and have a little fun while you're at it?"

Was that how people saw him and the company? As a bully? "I offer a fair price for the land. The buildings. There are no strong-arm tactics at work."

"Maybe that's how you see it." Zeke raised his beer, took a sip, then put it down again. "You oughta read the paper more often. Sometimes it gives you the side of the story you're not seeing."

Jake had little use for the media. He found most reporters intrusive, annoying and hardly interested in anything other than a sensationalized headline to splash across their pages. He called them when he needed press for a new launch, tried to stay under their radar the rest of the time. "I'm only concerned about the business section, Mr. Carson," he said.

"Zeke, please. Mr. Carson makes me sound like my father, and he's *old*."

Jake laughed. Despite everything, he found he liked Zeke. "Zeke it is."

Zeke finished his beer, then slid off the stool. He placed a firm hand on Jake's shoulder and met his gaze, with light blue eyes that had seen and experienced a lot of life. "I'm not here to tell you if your plans for this town are good or bad. There are arguments on both sides of the fence for that, and enough people to battle it out to start World War Three. But take some advice from a young-at-heart newspaperman." He glanced around the bar, not to see if anyone was listening, but as if he was trying to include the Clamshell Tavern in his case. "There are people whose whole lives are Harborside, and what you're proposing will turn their lives upside-down. I've seen and read about the kinds of hotels your company builds, and they may not be the right ones for here. Change isn't always a good thing, and you have to think about what's going to happen *after* you build this thing and head back to your big glass office in New York."

"What do you mean?"

Zeke pointed out the window, at a ship cutting through the cold ocean. "See that boat? It's plowing forward, on to its destination. It doesn't think about what happens in its wake. What the propeller is doing to the fish, the seaweed, all the flora and fauna living in the dark water underneath. That's why those channel markers are out there, to keep the boats in line. Keep them from destroying nature."

"And I'm the big bad boat, ripping up the seaweed in my wake, is that it?"

"You can choose to be, or you can choose to be a sailboat, leaving the ocean more or less as you found it." Zeke gave Jake's shoulder one last pat. "Think about it."

The old man left, and Jake turned back to his drink. Well, he'd been given a warning and a philosophy lesson, all at once. Seemed this town didn't want him around. Jake didn't care. He saw a business opportunity here, one he needed, on a professional and a personal level, and he had no intentions of walking away from it.

Outside the window, he saw Mariabella Romano striding up the boardwalk toward the Clamshell Tavern. As he watched her, he realized something he hadn't noticed before.

She had a way about her that didn't seem to fit this town. Heck, this world. It was more than the accent, the exotic beauty. She carried herself straight and tall, spine absolutely in line, as if she were balancing a book on her head and her stride—well, that could almost be called…

Regal. Yeah, that was the word for it.

Maybe she'd gone to one of those finishing schools or grown up in a wealthy home. Either way, she didn't fit his image of a small-town art gallery owner.

She entered the tavern, then the bar, her fiery gaze lighting on him as if he were the devil incarnate. A grin slid across his face. "Miss Romano. Just the person I wanted to talk to. I have an offer for you."

"And I have one for you." She crossed her arms over her chest. "I would like to pay you to leave Harborside, and find another town for your hotel. Name your price, Mr. Lattimore, and I will pay it."

Just when Jake had thought things couldn't get more interesting—

They did.

CHAPTER FOUR

It was an incredible risk, and Mariabella knew it.

But if money was what it would take to rid Harborside of Jake Lattimore, then she would take that chance. She had resources she could dip into—not an endless pool, of course, but probably more than enough to get this man to change his course. "So," she said, "what is your price?"

He chuckled. "You couldn't pay it. Not unless you have a few masterpieces in the back of your gallery that I don't know about."

"I have the resources I need to make this offer," she said, leaving the issue of where the money was coming from out of the discussion.

He leaned an elbow on the bar and studied her, clearly amused. She shifted under his scrutiny. How long had it been since a man stared at her like that, with such clear interest?

Not just the kind that said he found her intriguing as a woman, but that he saw her as a puzzle, something he wanted to study, read, get to know better.

A charge of electricity ran through the air, and Mariabella's stance faltered. She locked her ankles, then her knees, then her spine. Then her resolve.

This man would not affect her.

At all.

"I have to admit, this is an offer I've never heard before."

His grin widened. She didn't respond to the smile. "I'll have to think about it."

Good. Maybe he'd give her a figure and she could settle this. He met her gaze. "I've thought about it."

"For what, three seconds?"

"I'm not a man who takes long to make a decision."

She let out a gust. "That, I figured."

"And I've decided…" He paused. "No amount of money is going to change my mind."

"What?" Mariabella stared at him. Surely, she'd heard him wrong. "Surely, there must be—"

"No. Sorry."

Just like that. Two words. He'd refused her offer without even giving it serious consideration. Mariabella resisted the urge to shout in frustration. Surely there had to be something that would convince this man Harborside wasn't the right town for him.

"Why are you sure this town is the place for your hotel?"

"I've done my research and the numbers add up."

She shook her head. "So that is what Harborside is to you, a bunch of numbers?"

"Of course. I'm a businessman, Miss Romano. Only a fool would build a project using emotion as his barometer."

And in that answer, Mariabella knew the key to ridding the town of one Jake Lattimore. If she could get him to see the heart of Harborside, make him understand that this town mattered to the people who lived here, people like her, then perhaps, just perhaps, she could get Jake Lattimore to build an emotional connection with Harborside.

And then he couldn't possibly go through with his plans to ruin her sanctuary.

Right?

Maybe. She saw only one flaw in her plan. A man like Jake Lattimore probably had no heart, and wouldn't be swayed by an emotional appeal like this. Either way, she intended to try. After all, she'd fallen in love with this town on her first visit.

Maybe he would, too.

"Then I have another offer for you," she said, and her gut tightened as the words slipped out of her throat. This one was even riskier than the first offer she'd made. This one involved opening herself up to another person, making herself vulnerable. Risking—

Her identity.

No, she could be careful. She wouldn't talk about herself, only Harborside.

"And what are you offering this time?" he said with a smirk. "A famous sculpture in addition to cash on the table?"

"No." She took a step forward, ignoring the butterflies raising havoc in her gut. "I am offering me."

Jake had heard her wrong.

He was sure he had. No way Mariabella had just offered herself as a payment to send him packing. Although, stranger things did happen in business, and maybe she was serious. No. She couldn't be. This woman was too...

Uppercrust. Too proper in her demeanor, her language, her movements, to be the kind who'd sleep with a man merely to get him to call off a business deal. Right?

"You're seriously offering yourself?"

She nodded. "As your personal tour guide of Harborside. To show you the reasons why it's perfect the way it is."

He chuckled, half relieved she didn't mean she'd intended to sleep with him and half disappointed. "Why it doesn't need the big, bad hotelier, you mean."

"Exactly."

He considered that, his gaze connecting with hers as he thought over her offer. It was insane. He never got personal on a deal. Hadn't his father taught him that? When they got personal, the company suffered. It was only by staying on the corporate track, thinking with dollars and cents, that profits soared and megacorporations got built.

Lawrence Lattimore had drilled that lesson into his son for years. Had repeated it over and over again as he'd trained and groomed his son to take over the CEO spot. Don't get to know the locals, don't try to think about the people. Concentrate solely on the bottom line. Lawrence had lamented, several times, the mistakes he'd made in letting his heart rule his brain. Don't do it, he'd warned his son. Think like a CEO, not a person.

Get in, get the papers signed, then move on to the next town, the next project.

If Jake agreed to this, he'd be breaking the one sacred rule he'd been taught—never mix business with pleasure. Only an idiot would tell himself that taking the scenic route through Harborside beside a woman as beautiful as Mariabella Romano would be anything other than pleasurable.

He should be smart. He should leave this bar, get back to work on convincing the locals to sell their shops to him, so the plans for the hotel and condos could move forward. He had too much at stake to screw up this deal. Once Harborside was secure, Lattimore Properties could begin to return to the profitability it had enjoyed, and Jake would have earned the respect of the board.

Then he could fly to San Francisco. Fill his days with the next property. And the one after that. He kept hoping that one day, he'd finally find enough—

Enough work. Enough time away from his apartment. Enough time spent with those inanimate objects Will chided him about.

Enough—

To forget. To be able to move on. To have a life again.

Jake opened his mouth to say no to Mariabella, to tell her

he didn't have the time for such a senseless excursion, then his gaze connected with Mariabella's deep green eyes. Heat grew in the space between them, an awareness uncoiling like a rope. For a second, he saw only her. Not his job, not the papers waiting in his briefcase.

Just her eyes. Her smile.

How long had it been since he'd connected with someone? With a woman, at that? How long had it been since he'd anticipated spending time with a woman and thought of something other than work?

Too damned long.

He rose, put out his hand and closed the gap. When she took his hand, a surge of electricity ran through him.

Before his better judgment could say no, he said, "It would be my pleasure."

"Better button on," Mariabella said, "for our first stop."

"Button on?" Jake gave her a curious look.

She cursed her phrasing. It took a second for her brain to make the connections and find the right word choices, a fact she blamed entirely on her richly appointed surroundings. Plush leather interior, heated seats, even a small wine refrigerator at her feet. When Jake Lattimore bought a limo, he apparently did it right. Christmas music flowed softly from the stereo system, the sound of such high quality she could swear Jake had an entire orchestra in the trunk of the limousine.

She had, of course, been in a limo before. Hundreds of times. Not in the past year and a half, but her entire childhood and teen years had been spent living the life everyone expected of her. That meant dressing the way they thought she should. Living where they thought she should. And yes, even riding in what they thought she should. All to give off the proper image, because Lord knew, her life had been all about images.

Whether or not those images matched the woman inside hadn't mattered, not as long as the people were happy.

"I meant button up," Mariabella said, pushing the thoughts to the side. "It's cold outside, and you do not want to get sick."

He chuckled. "I haven't been sick in years, and even if I was, I wouldn't take the day off. I think my father would have a heart attack if I called in sick."

"Really?"

"I mean that rhetorically. He's gotten so used to seeing me at work every day, that if I ever stopped, it would be a shock. He counts on me to be there, because I'm the one taking over the company now that he's retiring and..." Jake sighed. "There are just a lot of expectations that come with being the one in charge. Like no sick days."

"I know what you mean. I used to be in a similar situation." She should have stopped herself before she said that. What was it with this man? Every time she was around him, she said more than she meant to, as if the brakes on her mouth stopped working.

He arched a brow, studying her. "How so?"

The limo pulled to a stop, and Mariabella tugged on the silver handle the instant the locks clicked. "Here we are!" She stepped out of the car so fast, the door nearly slammed into the chauffeur's gut. "Sorry."

"Happens all the time, ma'am." He gave her a grin. "Though most of the time, it's women running *to* Mr. Lattimore, not *from* him. I'm Will Mason, by the way, should you need anything."

Jake came around the car and gave the chauffeur a clap on the shoulder. "Are you filling her head with nonsense about me, Will?"

"Of course not." Will leaned toward Mariabella. "Only the truth."

Jake laughed, an easy sound that she hadn't heard from him before. "As long as you don't mention that time in Tallahassee, you'll stay on the payroll."

Will made a motion of zipping his lip, then winked at Mariabella.

"William..."

"I wouldn't dare tell her how you paraglided into that poor woman's hotel room." Will made a surprised *O* and covered his mouth, but his twinkling eyes belied the gesture. The two men clearly had a more friendly relationship than simply employer and employee. Mariabella had never seen any of the palace staff ever talk to her father like that. If they had, they would have been dismissed on the spot.

She envied Will and Jake's camaraderie. If she'd had a friend in the palace like that, even one, maybe all those long, boring days would have been more tolerable.

"He was quite the flyer that night," Will added. "I think he chose the wrong career. Should have been in the air force, instead of business."

Mariabella glanced over at Jake. "That desperate to see your date?"

Jake scowled. "More like I had troubles with the controls. First time in the air."

"Don't let him fool you. Mr. Lattimore has an adventurous streak that he keeps under wraps," Will said.

"Remind me again why I sign your checks," Jake said.

"Because I'm the only one who can keep up with you on a Jet Ski." Will shivered a bit in the cold. "When I can get you to take time to ride one, which better be soon after making me come to this clone of Alaska."

Mariabella watched the exchange, both surprised and amused. Surprised because Will mentioned that Jake had an adventurous side. Somehow, she couldn't quite see that with this business-only CEO. Secondly, amused because the two men had a repartee that spoke of a long-time friendship, something that showed another aspect to Jake Lattimore.

An aspect she could like, under different circumstances.

"And you can beat me at poker, Will," Jake chuckled again, "but we won't talk about that, either."

"Of course not." Will grinned, then disappeared back inside the driver's side of the limousine, leaving Jake and Mariabella alone. Five minutes ago, this tour of Harborside had seemed like a good idea, but now, out of the cocoon of her gallery, and far from the company of friends, Mariabella's awareness of Jake Lattimore doubled. The way he stood at least a head taller than her, how his shoulders filled his coat, defining the strong *V* of his torso. And most of all, how long it had been since she'd been kissed. Held. Loved.

Jake closed his cashmere overcoat, and fastened the buttons, as the winter wind off the ocean began to kick up. "Well, we're here. At the first stop on your guided tour. What exactly are we seeing?"

Get back to the point, Mariabella. Harborside, not him.

"That." She pointed up, at the top of the black-and-white oblong building beside them.

"The Harborside Lighthouse? I've seen lighthouses before, Miss Romano and—"

"You haven't seen this one." She grabbed his hand, intending only to lead him inside and cut off his protests, but when she touched him, a rush of heat ran through her. She jerked back, and hurried over to the door of the lighthouse. Away from him, and away from the temptation touching him seemed to bring. A quick double knock, then she stepped back to wait.

"Why aren't we going inside?"

"We have to wait for Cletus." She didn't turn around, even though she could sense Jake right behind her. Inches away. The heat of his body mingled with hers. And it felt nice.

Too nice.

"Cletus?" he asked.

"The lighthouse keeper."

"There are still people who do that?"

The note of surprise in his voice made her turn around. As soon as she did, she regretted it, because Jake was so close—the stoop was small, after all, only about three feet square, and sharing the space meant close quarters. "Harborside is a traditional town," she said. Concentrate on the tour, not him.

"Old-fashioned. Behind the times."

"Happy just the way it is."

"If you say so." He gave the rocky shoals around the lighthouse a passing glance, clearly not seeing what Mariabella did. The isolation of the area, the sweet quiet. The utter peace. "I thought lighthouses sat on rocks in the middle of the water."

"Some do. And some are on the coast, used to guide the boats into the harbor. To find their way home." The last word escaped her on a breath. Home.

When she had to return to Uccelli in two more months, if she ever had a chance to come back to Harborside, would that lighthouse guide her back? Most of all, would Harborside still feel like home, still wrap around her with the same comfort?

The door opened on creaky hinges, and a small wizened man peeked his head out. "Better be a damned good reason for you to bother me in the middle of the day," he said.

"And hello to you, too, Cletus," Mariabella said. "Glad to see you are in such a happy mood, what with Christmas just around the corner."

The older man scowled. "Where's my muffins?"

Mariabella propped a fist on her hip. "They will be here Christmas morning, and not a day sooner. And only if you promise to be nice, and come to Christmas Eve dinner with the rest of the family."

Cletus grumbled something under his breath, but opened the door and motioned the two of them inside. "Who's this character?"

"Jake Lattimore, this is Cletus Ridgemont, who for some reason I do not understand—" she winked at Cletus "—did not want to serve on the Welcome New Neighbors to Harborside Committee." Mariabella grinned, then waved between the two men. "Jake is here from out of town, and he wanted to see the view from the lighthouse."

Cletus looked Jake up and down, as if assessing his worthiness to enter the lighthouse. "You treating her nice?"

"Uh, yes, sir." Under Cletus's scrutiny, Jake had a moment of being back in high school, and enduring the inquisition by his dates' fathers. Only this wasn't a date and Cletus wasn't Mariabella's father. Was he? She'd mentioned family. Surely this odd character had no relation to her.

"Good. Our Mariabella deserves the best." Cletus wagged a finger at Jake. "You two go on up, but don't let him touch nothin'. He don't look like the lighthouse-keeper type and I don't want him breakin' my light."

Mariabella grinned. "Thank you, Cletus. We will only be a minute."

"Is that all you're wearing?" Cletus asked, motioning toward Mariabella's white wool coat.

"I'll be fine."

"You take my coat," he said, grabbing a thick khaki parka from a hook by the door. "And you wear it, you hear? Don't need you getting sick before Christmas. Who'll make my muffins if you do?"

Mariabella smiled, then shrugged into the second coat over her own. "Thank you."

Cletus only scowled, but Jake could see a softening in the man's features. He turned away, grumble-grumbling beneath his breath some more.

For all his bluster, the man clearly held a lot of affection for Mariabella. A twinge of envy ran through Jake. He'd been stuck in his office too long, that was for sure, if he was getting sentimental about a gruff lighthouse keeper who thrust his coat onto people.

"This way," Mariabella said, waving Jake toward a circular staircase dominating the room and spiraling toward the top of the lighthouse. Cletus's sparse living room surrounded the staircase, laid out in typical bachelor style. A bare-bones kitchen fed into a living room decorated with a single sofa and a plain maple end table. A TV sat atop a crate and a small oak bookshelf overflowed with paperback suspense novels.

Jake paused to look up the stairs—what appeared to be a thousand of them. The lighthouse had to be a hundred feet tall, and every foot would be climbed by them, not an elevator.

"Ready?" Mariabella asked, taking his hand. Every time she touched him, a surge of electricity ran through Jake, jolting long-dead senses back to life. Parts of him he'd thought had been shut off five years ago reawakened. He hadn't thought he could open his heart or feel that kind of hope again.

Not since—

Not since the future he'd planned had been crushed beneath a tractor trailer on the George Washington Bridge.

"Uh…yeah," he said.

Mariabella released him and started climbing the stairs, and Jake went back to being all business. Every ounce of him slipped back into that persona, as if he'd shed the coat of one man and put on the jacket of another.

The one of the more sensible man. The one who didn't get wrapped up in distractions he couldn't afford.

Except no matter how hard he tried, he couldn't forget the feeling of her touch, how her hand had been delicate and small, the skin as soft as rose petals.

As Mariabella walked ahead of him, he couldn't help but notice her curves. The arches of her calves, the hourglass of her waist, the way her hair hung in dark brown waves nearly to the small of her back. He reached up a hand, aching to run his fingers through those tresses.

He jerked his hand back. Business only. Stay on track. He

was here, not to fall for her or her town, but to utilize this time to sway Mariabella Romano over to his side, to make her understand how a Lattimore Resort could revitalize this sleepy little town.

All business—with no extracurricular activities. He had no intentions of returning to New York with anything other than a handful of signed deeds.

The wrought-iron staircase narrowed with each step, and when they reached the top of the stairs, they were standing in an enclosed, slightly musty space, with rough stone walls, probably hand-hewn a hundred years ago. Above their heads, the wooden ceiling had a small opening, with a ladder Jake guessed they were meant to climb to get to the final destination.

"We have to go up that?"

"You have already climbed a hundred feet, how difficult are a few more?" Mariabella tossed him a grin, then started up the ladder.

Giving Jake an exceptionally good view of her backside. For a moment, he couldn't remember exactly why he had objected to this idea in the first place. Why he had thought Mariabella Romano would bring trouble into his life.

Because right now she was bringing something very interesting to his day.

So much for business-only thoughts.

Jake shook his head and started up the ladder after her.

"Are you ready?" she called down to him.

"Ready for what?"

"The view of a lifetime." Mariabella smiled, then reached out a hand to help him over the edge. He should have refused the hand up—he didn't need it after all—but a part of him had started to look forward to touching her.

The part that hadn't realized he could look forward to a woman again. The part that had been buried in work for way too many years.

Jake shook his head. If he let his hormones rule his brain, he'd lose focus. He couldn't afford that, not now. Not with his career and the company's future riding on this deal.

Mariabella released his hand, and stood back. They were at the top of the lighthouse, beside a massive red lantern turning in a constant circle, and blinking every other second. "That thing's huge."

"I didn't bring you up here to see the beacon."

"Then what?" He glanced at his watch. He'd agreed to this excursion, but shouldn't have. He needed to get back to town and convince more people to sign over their properties to Lattimore. *That* was his priority. Not a lighthouse. And not a woman.

"This." She handed him a pair of binoculars and pointed out the glass windows.

He sighed. "Miss Romano—"

"Mariabella."

"Mariabella—" her name slid off his tongue like music, and the distraction started anew "—I don't have time—"

"Everyone has time for one look at the ocean, yes?" She gestured to him to peek through the lenses.

He lifted them to his eyes, and at first, saw nothing but blue. Mariabella leaned over and whispered in his ear, sending a rush of heat through his veins. "A little to the right."

When he shifted position, the circles of the binoculars filled with images of the ocean spreading around them in a vast circle of blue-green, rolling back and forth with choppy white-capped waves. Boats chugged through the channel, plowing through the water like a knife through melted butter. Jake shifted more to the right, and then, far off, he spotted a surge of black above the waves. It disappeared, then reappeared a few feet farther down. He glanced at Mariabella. "Is that…?"

A soft smile stole across Mariabella's face. "A whale. Yes, it is. I could stay here for hours and watch them. They're so incredible, are they not? Almost like…children."

"I'm not the poetry-in-motion kind, you know. I have a business to run." He began to lower the binoculars. "I really don't have time—"

"Shhh." Mariabella placed a finger over his lips, then withdrew it just as fast, as if the touch had seared her skin. "Stay a moment. No moving. No talking. Just…be."

Jake didn't know if it was the confined quarters of the beacon room, or the feel of Mariabella's finger on his lips, or the way she stood there, transfixed, but something in him caused him to take a moment, and breathe in the vast blue space around him.

The sky seemed to be kissing the ocean, and pouring its aqua beauty into the eagerly lapping waters below while a benevolent sun watched it all, and blessed the union with a golden dust. As Jake stood there, a weird sensation took over, first his limbs, then his senses. It was as if he couldn't—no, didn't want to—move.

For the longest time, he couldn't name the sensation. And then, finally he recognized the foreign feeling.

Peace.

"Look," Mariabella whispered, even though they were miles away and encased in a glass tower, "there he is again. And this time, he has a friend."

Jake leaned closer, peering through the salt-spattered glass for the flecks of black. "I don't see anything."

Mariabella shifted to the right, which brought her body within inches of his. She raised her arm and pointed. "There. Do you see him now?"

He saw a woman. With long, dark hair, and soft, soft skin. With every breath, he caught the scent of raspberries and almonds. And when Mariabella moved, as she did just then to look up at him, he fought a primal urge to kiss her.

For five years, he'd existed in a vacuum, and now this woman, this stranger, had stepped into the black hole of his life, like sunshine breaking over a horizon. She was making him set aside everything he should be thinking about.

Making him forget his priorities.

And right this second, he didn't care.

"It is incredible, yes?" she asked.

He watched her lips form the words. Felt them whisper across his skin. Heat rose in the space between them. Desire surged in Jake's chest. "Incredible."

Mariabella opened her mouth to say something else, then stopped. She swallowed. Her green eyes widened, her chest rose and fell, and Jake shifted just enough to close the gap between them.

Their torsos met, and a firestorm of attraction exploded in Jake's gut. Fire. He was playing with fire, and he knew where that led. To someone getting burned.

Step back, get back to business.

He shifted again, and their legs met. Her eyes widened even more.

"What…" she said, then let the sentence trail off.

Stop this before it starts. Be smart.

Jake reached up a hand, and caught one of those impossibly long, tempting tresses in his palm. Just as he'd imagined, the dark brown strands were silky smooth, and slid through his fingers with a whisper. "You were right."

She caught his hand, and met his gaze. "Right about what?"

"The view up here is amazing." He leaned closer, about to kiss her.

But instead, she laughed and stepped back. "Does every woman you meet fall for that one? Do they just collapse at your feet? Run *to* you, as Will said?"

He quirked a grin. "Most of them fall into my arms."

"You poor man." She shook her head again. "If you are done, Casanova, I have more of the town to show you."

"I'm done." Clearly, he'd been the only one who'd felt

anything in the air up here. Maybe it had been altitude sickness or maybe he really had been alone too long—and he'd forgotten how to read the subtle physical cues women sent.

As Mariabella turned and disappeared down the ladder, Jake took one last look out at the vast ocean. In the distance, he saw twin black humps crest, then disappear beneath the blue depths.

"Seems you're having better luck than me, Moby."

CHAPTER FIVE

THAT had been a close one.

Mariabella stuck to her side of the limo, as far from Jake Lattimore—and any potential for bodily contact—as possible. In the rearview window, she watched the Harborside Lighthouse grow smaller and smaller as they headed away from the rocky coastline and back toward town.

For a second in that tower, she'd actually made the mistake of thinking Jake was attracted to her. That he'd wanted her for *her.* For the real Mariabella.

Except he didn't know the real Mariabella, did he?

She clearly had let this American way of life soften her wits, because if she had been back in her own country, in her own element, she never would have fallen for such an obvious ploy to—

Well, to use and manipulate her.

This man was here to buy her building. To use her as an ally in his bid to buy the rest of the buildings on the block. His only interest in her came with dollar signs in his eyes.

Even if his intentions had been true, she had no business getting close to a man. Doing so meant being vulnerable. Opening up. Sharing parts of her past.

Like where she came from.

Why she was here.

And who she really was.

If there was a list of the top three things Mariabella never intended to tell anyone, those were them. The story she'd led people to believe was that she'd come to Harborside on vacation over a year ago and loved it so much, she'd decided to stay. From her accent, people assumed she was Italian, and she'd let those assumptions stand.

Better to let others fill in the blanks than to do that herself—whenever she opened her mouth, she left too much room for error. And so, Mariabella maintained as much distance in her personal relationships as she could, to avoid answering impossible questions. And she busied herself repaying people for their friendship with the skills she had— organizing town events that brought Harborside and that drew in more visitors. Not enough, clearly, if Harborside was vulnerable to a man like Jake Lattimore.

So she didn't talk about her past, her family, or her heritage. She kept her friendships on a surface level, never allowing anyone in too close.

Today, she'd made the mistake of forgetting her commitment to distance, and allowed Jake Lattimore to close the gap. For just a second, she'd let herself think that she was just like every other woman in this town.

One who could date, fall in love, live an ordinary future with a husband, children.

Instead of one living a lie. Instead of one who was living on a ticking clock, and who would be leaving soon to take her place on a throne. Until then her priority was this town, and keeping it out of greedy hands like Jake's.

He wasn't a date—he was the enemy.

Remember that, Mariabella.

"That house there," she said to Jake, pointing out the window as they rounded the corner, "is the oldest home in

Harborside. Built right around the time the founding fathers of America were writing the Declaration of Independence."

He arched a brow. "Who are not your founding fathers, I take it, because your accent definitely isn't native to this country."

She ignored the question. "If you notice the architecture, it has a Georgian style, but an addition was added in 1920—"

"Where are you from?" Jake interrupted. "Italy? Spain?"

"The people who added on didn't stay true to the original style of the building. So, in 1979, when the present owner bought the house—"

"Definitely from a region near Italy," he continued, as if she hadn't said a word. "I've been there several times, mostly on business, sadly. But I did have time for one short visit, a couple years ago."

"He decided to take down the addition and rebuild it from..." Her voice trailed off. They had passed the object of her little speech several minutes ago. "Coming up on your right—" Mariabella pointed past him and out the window, hoping to deflect his attention "—is the first church built in Harborside."

"Are you going to continue to avoid getting to know each other on a personal level?" Jake leaned forward, propping his elbows on his knees. The limo suddenly seemed as small as a subcompact.

"I see little point in it," she said, regardless of that little bit she had let slip earlier today. And that moment in the lighthouse. Both aberrations. She wouldn't make the same mistake twice. "You are here on business, and I am here to show you the wisdom of taking your business elsewhere."

"What if I'm interested in combining a little pleasure with my business?"

"Then I suggest staying at the Harborside Seaside Inn. They offer a spa service on weekends."

He chuckled. "Are you always this difficult?"

"No. Generally, I am quite pleasant." She offered him a smile as proof.

He returned her smile with one of his own. A smile that hit Mariabella squarely in the gut, sending the hormones that she'd managed to reduce to a slow simmer back up to a full boil.

The man had a heck of a nice smile, she'd give him that. The kind that curved up a little higher on one side than the other, giving him a touch of mischief behind his blue eyes. For a second, she wondered if he was, as Will had said, a man given to fun.

The kind who would say, "Hey, let's go scuba diving this weekend," and book them two tickets to Jamaica. The kind who would throw an impromptu picnic on the living room floor. The kind who would—

Who would bring the kind of fun into Mariabella's life that she had missed living in that caged fishbowl.

"Well, pleasant Mariabella Romano, let's see this church of yours." He pressed a button at his side, and the driver slowed, then pulled over. A moment later, they were out of the car and heading toward the tall white spires of the church.

"I thought you were no longer interested in my tour."

"If I'm going to invest in this town, I need to know as much about it as I can. From bagels to Bibles." He caught her gaze. "Wouldn't you agree?"

Somehow, she suspected he had managed to turn this around, back to his advantage. Mariabella was not used to being in this position. A monarch, even one in training, always maintained control. Always had the upper hand.

Those lessons had been bred into her, and drilled into her again and again over the years. As they headed up the granite stairs of the church, Mariabella vowed to put the very knowledge she had hated learning to use—and get this derailed train back on the right track.

Whether there was a nice smile in the way or not.

***

But an hour later, after taking Jake Lattimore through the church, down the block past the dozen or so historic homes that made up the center of Harborside, and then driving back to the boardwalk, she had to admit she had yet to regain her familiar footing at the top.

The sun had begun to set, dropping a blanket of deep orange across the Atlantic. A chill fell over the town, and Mariabella drew her coat tighter against winter's bite when she stepped out of the limo. "You enjoyed your tour of Harborside, Mr. Lattimore, did you not?"

"I did." He waved off the chauffeur, before Will could get out of the car. "And I don't want it to end."

Mariabella pivoted, gesturing toward the buildings they'd just seen. "I don't know of other landmarks, except the board-walk and you have—"

"I didn't mean that."

She turned back toward him. Jake's blue gaze held hers, steady and sure. He had a way of looking at a woman that pierced through the layers she'd put in place. The ones meant as keep-out signs, the ones that had worked so successfully with other men.

Every other man, it seemed, but this one.

"Then what do you mean?" she asked.

"I saw a sign back there for something I haven't done in a really long time. Something I suspect you haven't done either."

"If it's skiing, I assure you, I have—"

"The Christmas Dance at the town hall."

Her jaw dropped. She started to say a word, couldn't think of one, then tried again. Nothing.

He was asking her out? To a dance? On a date?

She had organized the dance with several other business owners in Harborside as a way to celebrate the holiday and bring together the townspeople. She had learned in the palace that celebrations had a way of reducing political tensions and forming new alliances among old foes. Something about the flow of wine and the music of laughter got people building bridges they wouldn't otherwise form.

"I haven't been to a dance myself since…probably high school," he went on. "It's a good way to get to know the townspeople in a more casual setting, and that will work toward my goal, too."

"Your goal?"

"I can change some of those negative impressions that I'm sure are springing up all over town like crocuses in April. And if you go with me," he said, grinning, "you can remind people behind my back how awful I am."

She cocked her head and studied him. "That is *against* your plans, is it not?"

"Ah, but it's part of another plan of mine." The grin widened. "I don't know about you, but I work much too many hours, and I could use a break."

"A break?" The echo escaped her in a whisper. Her concentration seemed to have flown south with the geese. This was bad. Very bad.

She was a princess, a royal—and a royal maintained order, both personal and national, no matter what. If she didn't, disaster would result.

Mariabella had heard this lesson from her father, spoken in his dispassionate, quiet voice, over and over again. Never allow passion to rule over logic. If you did, people got hurt.

People like her.

"I shouldn't—" she began.

"You should. Have some fun tonight, Mariabella."

Fun. He'd spoken the magic word. Wasn't that exactly what she'd been seeking all her life? The one thing she'd been denied? She'd grown up imprisoned by expectations and decorum—as the future queen, her prison was even tighter than that of her sisters'—and she'd always wished for someone, something to break her out.

She'd come to this town, hoping to find that escape, and instead been imprisoned in a different way. By her own lies. So she'd buried herself in her gallery, in helping the town, and backed away from personal relationships.

Now Jake Lattimore stood before her, offering the very gift she'd always wanted, like her own personal Santa.

Did she dare accept?

"Come on, Mariabella. Everyone deserves a break. That's just smart business." He took a step forward, buffeting her from the cold air, warming the space between them. But most of all, tempting her to use him as a shield from the long, cold days ahead. "That's what this would be. Business only."

"Business only? You have no ulterior motives at all?"

The smile quirked up a little higher on one side than the other. "Well, I may want to perfect my waltz while I'm at it."

Logic over passion. Never let her heart get ahead of her brain. If she could keep that in mind tonight, and use all that she had been taught to her advantage, then she'd be fine. She could do that and still have fun, couldn't she?

"All right, I will go with you," Mariabella said. And made a date with the enemy.

"What the hell are you doing?" Will asked, glancing at the flyer Jake had handed him, before tossing it onto the dash and putting the car in gear.

"Going to a dance. And working at the same time."

Will muttered something under his breath that sounded close to "idiot."

"Excuse me?"

"You should go to the dance, and *dance*. Not work at all." Will swung the limo through Harborside's streets and stopped in front of the town hall where the dance was being held, and

Jake had agreed to meet Mariabella. "There's a beautiful woman in there, and if you think about anything other than her legs tonight, then you need a lobotomy."

He had far too many things on his work plate right now to consider adding in a relationship. Will would tell him he was making an excuse. Again. The same excuse he'd made for the last five years.

Ever since he'd lost Victoria.

For a minute there in the lighthouse, he'd considered something else, but in the time since he'd dropped off Mariabella, he'd come back to his senses. "My mind will be on balance sheets, Will. Not anything *between* the sheets. I'll be back in an hour."

Will muttered something else a lot less flattering than "idiot."

"What?"

"Number one, you're at a dance, Jake. I don't know who taught you Dating 101, but that's the easiest way to get close to a woman without having to pay for dinner first."

Jake chuckled.

"And if you want to dance with her, you might want to change."

Jake looked down at his dark navy suit and blue striped tie. "What's wrong with what I'm wearing?"

"You look like you're heading to a convention for undertakers." Will unknotted his own tie and tossed it over the seat. The silk fabric unfurled in a cacophony of red, green and white. "Here. Wear mine."

"I'm not—"

"*Act* like a fun guy, Jake, and one of these days, you might just turn back into one."

Fun. The very thing he'd proposed to Mariabella earlier. Trouble was, Jake wasn't so sure he was ready for fun in his life again. It was far easier to stay in the familiar world of work. Jake reached for the door handle, then heard a familiar click.

"Wear the tie," Will said. "Surprise her. You might surprise yourself in the process. What's the worst that can happen?"

"For one, she might laugh her head off."

"So fire me, if she does. And if she kisses you instead, I want a raise." Will winked.

Kiss Mariabella Romano? Just the thought sent a roar of anticipation running through Jake. Today, he'd almost...

He pictured her lush lips beneath his, her curvy body in his arms, her thick dark hair tangled in his hands.

He changed his tie.

"Get involved," Will said before Jake got out of the car. "It won't kill you."

"Maybe," Jake said. "Maybe not."

Outside, a gust of winter wind cut down the sidewalk, cold, sharp, vicious. Jake inhaled, and drew his coat closed against the sudden frigid temperature. Mother Nature's fury held nothing over the ice binding his heart, a self-protective shield he'd thought would keep him from ever feeling that pain again.

But as he gripped the door handle to the Harborside Town Hall, he wondered if he was fooling himself. Did avoiding a topic mean it went away—or was he just killing time, filling those empty holes with balance sheets and architectural plans?

He entered the building, and was immediately greeted by a rock band belting out Christmas songs, a crowd of people filling the dance floor and milling about the perimeter of the room, and a burst of red and green decorations, broadcasting Christmas spirit loud and clear.

His gaze skipped over all of it. The logical, left side of Jake's brain told him to move around the room, to start networking, warm up the residents of Harborside, start convincing the more reluctant sellers that this deal was in their best interests. He had a limited window of time, after all, and every minute he wasted cost the company.

Except, he couldn't seem to focus on anything except finding Mariabella Romano. He scanned the room, seeking her familiar face, telling himself he'd start with her. She was the most logical choice, after all. Head of the Community Development Committee, and all that.

Uh-huh.

Then why did his pulse kick up a dozen notches when he spied her across the room? Why did he start weaving through the crowd, mumbling vague hellos to the half dozen or so people he'd already met in Harborside, instead of focusing on the job at hand?

"You look…stunning," he said when he reached Mariabella. The rest of the room dropped away, the space seeming to close in to just him. And her.

She'd accented her curves with an emerald sweater in a V-neck, decorated with rhinestones that peppered the front like snowflakes. A black skirt cut away from her knees in a swirl of ruffles, and drew his eye down to spiky black-and-silver high heels that only made her already amazing legs look even more amazing. She'd curled her hair, and piled it on top of her head in a riot of curls that begged a man to find every pin, and release the tendrils one by one.

"Thank you." A slight blush filled her cheeks. "Is that how you convince everyone to sell you their properties, Mr. Lattimore?"

"Please, call me Jake." He took a step closer, his gaze catching her green eyes, the color as deep and vibrant as a forest on a stormy day.

"Jake."

His name rolled off her tongue in a sweet song he'd never heard another woman sing. Impartiality kept yielding to testosterone, making it impossible to think about anything but kissing her.

Oh, he was in trouble.

She stepped forward and ran a finger down his tie. A smile curved across her face. "What's this?"

Her touch nearly sent him over the edge. He drew in a breath, fought the urge to take her in his arms. "A little Christmas spirit."

"I like it. You surprise me, Jake. I didn't think you were a snowman fan."

He sure as hell was now.

The band segued into a slow song, and couples began making their way onto the dance floor. Jake put out his hand. "Shall we?"

She hesitated, then nodded, took his hand and followed him out to the dance floor. Her palm was delicate, she had long, fine fingers, and when she put one hand on his back, the other still clasped inside his larger one, he thought how like a hummingbird she was. Fragile, yet strong, determined, and impossible to pin down.

"I thought this was business only," she said.

"It's Christmas. Surely we can have a little fun, too." Will would have laughed if he could have heard Jake right now.

They began to waltz in a slow, easy circle, Mariabella's steps surer and better than his. Clearly, she'd done this a time—or a hundred.

"You're not only beautiful, you're a wonderful dancer," he said.

"Is that how you get what you want in business? By sweet-talking the other side?"

He chuckled. "No. I don't usually call the people I'm in the midst of negotiating with 'stunning.'"

Her green eyes met his. "Is that what this is, a negotiation?"

"Isn't that what all dancing is? A negotiation?" Except he'd stopped doing any kind of business the minute he'd stepped on the dance floor. Something else had started between them, something far more serious and with far higher stakes than a real estate transaction.

He knew it. She knew it.

A smile curved across her face, lighting her eyes, and lighting a flame in Jake's gut, one he had thought died a long time ago. He found his hold on her tightening ever so slightly, his head dipping just a little, enough that if he wanted to, he could close the gap between them with a whisper—

And kiss her.

"If this is a negotiation," Mariabella said softly, "then that means one of is going to lose, yes?"

They stepped to the right, her body moving in perfect rhythm with his. Jake moved a half inch closer, and the silky ends of her hair brushed against his cheek. The scent of raspberries and almonds wafted up to tease at his senses. An errant curl had tugged loose from one of the bobby pins holding it in place, and Jake fought the urge to tug the tendril down, to let it slip through his fingers.

"Perhaps," he whispered, his voice nearly a growl, as desire roared in his gut, "we can compromise instead."

"You do not strike me as the type of man who compromises." She took a step forward, bringing her torso in contact with his for an all too brief second. Every sane thought in Jake's head disappeared.

"And what about you?" He slid his palm up her back and twirled her to the right. She didn't miss a step, matching him move for move. "Are you a compromiser, or a winner?"

"Oh, I am very accustomed to always getting exactly what I want," she said. "To people always doing what I tell them to."

"Pity."

"Why do you say that?"

"Because I am exactly the same way."

"Then it looks like we have a problem."

Her perfume intoxicated him. The curve of her neck riveted his attention, and every step she took knocked him off guard. For a man used to being in control, the feeling was new, unexpected. "Or maybe," Jake said, as the band began to sing the last few notes, "we'll find a way to make this work out for both of us."

The song ended, and the band announced they were taking a break. People began to leave the dance floor, and music from a CD player replaced the live instruments.

"Or maybe," Mariabella said, stepping away from him and breaking the spell between them, "one of us *will* win. Thank you for the dance, Mr. Lattimore. I think it will be smart if we stick to business instead of fun. Don't you agree?"

She headed for a table laden with appetizers and a massive bowl of red punch. He took two steps to follow her, then turned away.

And did the smart thing.

Got back to work.

What had she been thinking?

For five minutes, Mariabella had let herself get swept up in a dance, in a romantic moment, fooled into thinking the arms around her held interest in her, not her gallery. She'd forgotten the identity she'd worked so hard to protect, forgotten the life she'd built, and considered—

Considered kissing him.

Again.

Twice in one day.

She'd broken the cardinal rule her father had drilled into her. The one thing he had insisted on over and over, and made clear in the way he lived his life and interacted with his family.

Reason over emotion. Never, ever let your desires do the thinking for you. That was the kind of mistake that started wars, for goodness sake.

"He must be a Leo," Carmen whispered in her ear.

"A what?" Mariabella asked, turning away from the dance

floor, and focusing on the trays of food, even though her appetite had disappeared.

"You know, the astrological sign? He's like a lion on the prowl tonight."

"I have no idea who you are talking about."

Carmen propped a fist on her hip. "Did you just dance with Mr. Invisible? Because I thought I saw you waltzing around the floor with Prince Charming a second ago."

"He is no prince. Trust me, I know. And far from charming."

Carmen leaned against the table and watched Jake cross the room. "Sure looks like every prince I've read about in a fairy tale. Tall, dark, handsome—"

"Incredibly boorish, self-centered and after one thing."

"A beautiful princess?"

The word hit Mariabella with the force of a rogue wave. She swallowed hard and glanced away for a second, hoping that surprise didn't show on her face. "Well, he should look elsewhere." A skittish laugh escaped her.

"Why? I mean, you're *here*."

"What?" Alarm raised the pitch in the word.

Carmen draped an arm around her boss. "In case you haven't noticed, you are a very eligible catch. I've even heard Cletus say he'd marry you and that guy is the biggest hermit to come along since Bigfoot."

Mariabella laughed. "Cletus? He just likes my cooking."

"Come on, Mari. You're gorgeous. You have that accent thing going on, and you're…mysterious."

"Did they spike the punch this year?" Mariabella asked. Change the subject. Get the focus on something other than herself and mysteries to be solved. "I think I'll try a cup and see."

"Men love that stuff," Carmen went on. "They love women who are a puzzle."

Mariabella ladled some punch into cup. Gulped half of it down. "No. No liquor."

"Let me give you one hint about guys. You don't want to play Mystery Woman for too long."

"Did you see these cookies? They are like little Christmas trees. Cute, yes?" Mariabella grabbed one but didn't eat it.

Carmen didn't move off topic. "It's like doing the Sunday crossword. That sucker's hard. Eventually you give up because you get frustrated. Unless you're like a genius, and then maybe you stick it out. Most of us, we just let it go after twenty-nine down, know what I mean?"

"Jake Lattimore is the puzzle, not me," Mariabella said.

Carmen grinned. "A lot of women wouldn't mind figuring out what's making him run across and down."

"Easy. He wants to buy this town." Mariabella wagged a cookie in Carmen's direction. "Do not let his smile fool you."

"So you *did* notice his smile."

"Only because he insists on using it as a lethal weapon."

Carmen laughed. "He's not that bad."

"He wants to take over Harborside, Carmen. What is good about that?"

Carmen leaned in to Mariabella and lowered her voice. "Did you ever think this town could use some extra oomph? That maybe its destiny is to become something more than a sleepy little place for people to work on their tans in the summer?"

"You have no idea how that could ruin a place," Mariabella said. "How a man like him can destroy a perfect world."

"I've been reading his auras, Mariabella, and I think his intentions are all for good. You should—"

"No," Mariabella said, interrupting Carmen before she could add another argument to the pile. Or worse, return to the Prince Charming and princess matchmaking conversation. That could lead to nothing good. "What I should do is gather the Harborside business owners together so we can come up with a plan to stop him. Before it's too late."

CHAPTER SIX

HE WATCHED them leave, one after another, following Mariabella Romano out of the room like chicks behind a mother duck. Every one of the people he had talked to that morning left the dance.

He leaned against the wall and smiled.

Well, hell. She was a step ahead of him, and he admired that. It had been a while since he'd met such a challenge—on a personal and business level.

Not to mention such a mystery. He'd spent an entire day with Mariabella Romano and knew less about her than he knew about the doorman who worked at Lattimore Properties.

And that guy just started working for the company last week.

Jake rubbed his chin, and plotted a new strategy. Looked like he had an uprising in the making. He had to get creative.

And that meant outflanking Miss Romano, before she did the same to him.

Except, this time, a part of him resisted. Somewhere deep inside Jake, a rebellion had started, a whisper telling him to back away. To let this project go. To let Mariabella keep her town just as it was.

Why?

He'd never done that before. Never treated anything he'd

pursued with kid gloves. This was business, pure and simple. Heart didn't figure into the equation.

That was dangerous thinking. *Bad* thinking. He had to nip that in the bud and quick. No way was he going to deviate from the plan, from the proven formula.

His father would never approve of him thinking with anything resembling sentimentality. Once upon a time, Lawrence Lattimore had been a man who'd run his company with his emotions. But as he'd told Jake over and over, he hadn't gotten rich until he'd left his heart on the curb and started thinking with his brains.

And neither would Jake. No. He'd convince Mariabella Romano that a Lattimore Resort was a good thing for this town—and do it in a way she'd never forget.

A half hour later, Mariabella reentered the room, her business owner ducks again following, then dispersing. The band had started up again, launching into a rousing rendition of a popular Christmas carol. Someone in a snowman suit climbed onto the stage and began gyrating along to the song, boogying close enough to the cymbals to provide an extra clash here and there.

Jake crossed to Mariabella, his pulse kicking up as the gap between them closed. Damn. She had a certain mystique about her, like a veil blocking anyone from seeing the real woman. Even as he fought his attraction to her and told himself to stick to business, the rest of his body mutinied.

"I'd like to make you an offer," he said.

Wariness filled her gaze. "An offer?"

"Come with me tomorrow. And let me show you what a Lattimore resort can be like. Find out firsthand what my company can bring to Harborside." She began to protest, but he put up a finger and laid it against her lips. When he touched her mouth, a surge of desire roared through him. He lowered his hand.

"I can't possibly leave. I have an opening in two days and—"

"You have an assistant. Let her assist."

"I—"

"If you want to battle the enemy, what better way to do so than to see exactly what you're up against?"

He would give her a visual image—one she couldn't argue with. Let her see the dollars and sense in his designs. In one of the diamonds of the Lattimore jewelry case. Then surely all her arguments about a megahotel would disappear.

She considered him. "All right, I'll go. But do not think I can be persuaded by a fancy room or a steak dinner. I am not like other women. At all."

Then she walked away, leaving Jake even more mystified than he had been when the evening started.

Who *was* this woman? And where exactly had she come from?

Mariabella loved mornings. But not early mornings.

She stood outside the gallery, shivering in her winter coat, at a few minutes before four, and wondered what insanity had driven her to agree to Jake Lattimore's proposal last night. The dark wrapped around her with an icy chill, the boardwalk eerily quiet, everything still closed up for the night. Behind her, the ocean whooshed back and forth, whispering its constant music.

The limo glided down the street, tires crackling on the half-frozen road. Mariabella didn't wait for Will to open her door. She hopped inside and closed the door, glad to be cocooned in the heated leather interior.

"I would have been happy to pick you up in front of your house," Jake said.

She knew Jake Lattimore had no idea who she really was, but still, she wanted to put as many layers of protection between herself and her true identity as she could. Hence, meeting him at the gallery this morning. "I had some work to do before I left."

"You sound like me. No time for a personal life."

She laughed. "Small business owner. It goes with the territory."

"It's the same for big business owners." He handed her a cup of coffee, and she thanked him. "What do you know? We have something in common."

Mariabella simply sipped her coffee. The blend was hearty but wonderful. The rich, warm aroma helped awaken Mariabella's senses, and draw her into the land of the living, despite the ridiculously early hour. "I can't believe you found coffee this early."

"We brought it with us."

"You brought your own coffee?"

"I like what I like, and I didn't want to bother the B and B owner this early. Will brewed it for us at the inn this morning before we left." He gestured toward a silver carafe sitting on the small table to the right.

The joys of having exactly what you wanted when you wanted it—how Mariabella missed that. She loved living in Harborside, but there were aspects of palace life that she did miss. Being able to call down to the kitchen at two in the morning because she had a sudden craving for pizza. Waking up to breakfast in bed every morning. Having someone there to tend to everything she needed—from new shoes to making the bed.

Of course, that had all come at a price. A lack of privacy. Her entire life dictated from the day she was born. A public face she could never stop wearing. She'd brew her own coffee, thank you very much, and have her life to herself.

"Where are we going?" she asked.

"If I told you, it wouldn't be a surprise." He grinned, then shifted in his seat to face her. "I have only one rule for this trip. We don't talk about Harborside or the argument we're having about its future for the entire trip. Instead, we act like—" he paused, and met her gaze "—friends."

Mariabella nearly spit out her coffee. "Friends? You? And me?"

"Am I that much of an ogre?"

She bit back a smile at his choice of words. If he only knew who she was, he wouldn't reference fairy-tale creatures. "No. Not an ogre."

"Then is it that unbelievable that you and I could be friends under different circumstances?"

Her gaze locked with his blue eyes. A shiver of awareness ran through her, and she thought of the moment in the lighthouse. How close they had come to kissing. How much she had *wanted* him to kiss her. How lonely she had been over the last year, heck, her whole life. She hadn't been seen as just Mariabella, as an ordinary woman living an ordinary life, by any man.

Until now.

She had a chance, for a few hours, to sit and play the game. To pretend. Would that be so bad?

"Perhaps not so unbelievable," she said.

A smile curved along his face, feeding the desire that had been coiling in her gut with the memory of that near kiss. When he smiled, it lit up his eyes, crinkled along the corners, and made her wonder—

What if?

"So what do non-ogre friends talk about?" she asked.

He laughed. "Well, for starters, where did you grow up?"

Under any other circumstances, with any other person, that question would be ordinary. Something that wouldn't send out the palace guards on a rescue mission. Or the media on a "find the princess" frenzy. There was no way to answer that with the truth, not if she wanted to keep her identity secret. "Along the coast of Italy," she said finally. A small lie. Uccelli was north of Italy's coast.

"From your accent, I assumed that. I've traveled there. Beautiful country."

"And you?" she asked, before he could probe deeper into her past. "Did you always live in New York?"

"I've never known another home, if you can call an apartment a home."

"And you do not."

He shrugged. "It's a place to lay my head at night. When I'm there."

"I know how that feels," she said quietly. Darn. How did that slip out?

"Isn't Harborside a home for you?"

"It is the closest thing to home I've ever known." That was the truth. She could feel the smile filling her face, the joy she'd found in the tiny seaport exploding in the gesture. "I love it there."

"You didn't love your life in Italy?"

"I was not—" she paused, choosing her words carefully "—as happy there. As...comfortable, not like I am in Harborside."

"You're lucky." His gaze went to the window, and she wondered if he was watching Harborside in the distance, or something else. "I haven't found a place like that. And I've been all over the world."

"I think home is where you make it. I think I would have been just as happy in New York or California or London."

"Yet you didn't find home where you grew up."

"There were...other issues involved."

He arched a brow. "Like what?"

She peered at him over the rim of her coffee cup. "We are just friends getting to know each other, are we not? I do not have to tell all on the first trip."

"You are a mysterious woman, Mariabella."

Her name rolled off his tongue like a song. A craving to hear him say it again rose inside her, and she found herself leaning forward, as if moving nearer would make Jake repeat his words. "I thought men liked mystery."

"We do." A smile, a twinkle in his eyes. "Very much."

Flirting. They were flirting.

She should stop.

"And what about you?" she asked. "Do you like a woman with a little mystery?"

Jake paused a moment, then leaned closer. He reached up and caught a tendril of her hair between his fingers. She held her breath, her heart pounding a furious beat. "I didn't think I did." A second passed. He let the tendril of hair slide through his fingers. "Until now."

Desire roared inside her. Her gaze locked on his eyes, then his mouth. Her thoughts drifted to what those lips could do, given half a chance. Oh, my. "Then I suppose I should stay mysterious."

Why had she said that? Why hadn't she backed away?

She needed to stay uninvolved. Unencumbered. It was the only way to protect the freedom she had worked so hard to achieve.

And yet…

His touch drifted along her cheek now, and she forgot to breathe, forgot her name. "It's been a long time since I've had to unravel a puzzle," he said.

"Me, too."

"Am I a puzzle to you?"

She nodded. Her voice seemed to have gone south, too.

"How is that? I thought most men were pretty easy to figure out."

"Your intentions are…not always so clear." Like whether he wanted just the land in Harborside, or whether he wanted her, too. Or whether this whole seduction scene was merely an attempt to talk her into signing on the dotted line.

"It is getting a little muddled, isn't it?"

She nodded again.

"Then let's stick to just the ride." He sat back against his seat, and disappointment filtered into the space between them.

She should have been happy. She should have been thrilled to return to her comfort zone, the one that didn't involve the encumbrance of a relationship.

Except the empty spots in her heart, her life, kept crying out for someone else to bring another dimension to her days and nights. Someone who understood her. Who knew the real Mariabella.

Ha. That would mean starting with telling a man who she really was. And she couldn't do that, not without giving up everything that mattered.

The rest of the ride, she and Jake exchanged small talk, as if both of them had decided to maintain their distance. He took several calls; she pulled a sketch pad out of her purse, and kept herself busy making drawings of the landscape around them, as the sun came up and kissed the winter land with light.

A few hours later, they crossed into New York City. The buildings and noise surrounded them in an instant, a cacophony of noise and color. Mariabella set her sketchbook aside and sat back, taking in the view, enthralled by the massive skyscrapers, the congestion of people, the burst of holiday decorations on every building, every street corner.

"Have you been here before?"

"Twice," she said, not explaining both trips had been state business with her father, never vacations. "But every time, it is like seeing New York all over again."

"Then we'll have to return when we have more time," he said.

She glanced back at Jake, trying to read the meaning in those words. But his gaze was on the view outside, and not on her.

A few minutes later, William stopped the limo in front of an elaborate hotel, seated across from Central Park. The Lattimore Resort and Hotel had the appearance of being trimmed in gold, and featured four-story columns, and a two-story all-glass front door that revealed a marble foyer and massive water fountain inside.

Jake made a long-winded speech, explaining the hotel's virtues, listing its rooms, its five-star spa, its technologically advanced business center. "It's one of the best Lattimore Resorts available, and we'd bring a lot of these features to Harborside, so that many of the upscale clientele could find these same amenities when they go on a small-town vacation."

"It is certainly impressive," Mariabella said.

Jake put up a finger, motioning for William to wait before getting out to open the doors. "But you don't love it."

"Well…I don't mean to be rude, but anyone can build a hotel. Even an impressive one. I've stayed in many like this one."

"And would you stay in this one?"

She shrugged. "Perhaps."

"I hear a 'but' in that sentence." He draped an arm over the back of the seat and studied her. "What is it?"

"Jake, we drove all these hours and miles. I do not want to criticize your hotel before I have seen it. We should go in, and I will give it a fair view."

"You've seen enough to make a judgment, though, haven't you?"

She wanted to lie. Thought about lying. But really, where would that get her? And him? "I…" She sighed. "I simply like something different."

He chewed that over for a minute. "But this is what we have planned for Harborside."

"I know." She placed her palm against the window, as if she could block the hotel, which reminded her so much of the castle. "Don't you have anything…simpler?"

"All of our resorts are like this. Studies show—"

She wheeled toward him. "I do not read studies. I read in here." She laid a hand on her heart. "And there must be something else. Something less…gaudy."

He rubbed at his chin, thinking about her words for so long, Mariabella was sure she had offended him. She shouldn't have said a thing. After all, if someone had come in and criticized her gallery, she would have been upset. Jake probably felt the same way about his hotel. It would have been better just to exclaim over every feature and leave it at that.

Hadn't she learned to be polite? To keep her opinions to herself? A princess didn't voice her opinions, not in front of others. A princess was, above all, polite and sweet. Never disparaging, never disagreeable.

And always, always diplomatic.

She touched Jake's hand. "We can go inside. I am sure this is a lovely hotel with a great deal to offer your guests."

"No." He shook his head. "You made very valid points. And I happen to agree with them, even if the research shows otherwise. I just happen to be a guy who likes a different kind of vacation experience."

She laughed. "Me, too. This—" she waved toward the hotel "—is not my idea of a vacation."

He nodded. "Then let me show you something else." He picked up a phone beside him and told Will to start driving again. The limo pulled away from the curb and glided down the road.

"Well, I had hoped that building would impress you."

She shook her head. "I am sorry. I am a simple person. I like home and what do you call it…? Hearth. If you had something like that, maybe then—"

Jake grabbed the phone again. "Will, do you remember that place in New Jersey?" He paused. "Yeah, that's the one. Let's go there." Another pause. "I know, I know, but I can call in a favor and we can get in there."

"Where are we going?"

"Somewhere that has home and hearth. A lot of it." Jake glanced out the window and watched New York rush by. "This city may be my address, but where I'm taking you, that's the only place I ever felt at home."

Woodsmoke curled from the chimney and scented the air with hickory. Two white rocking chairs on the long wrap-around porch waved lazily in the chilly breeze. Snowdrifts danced in waves across the lawn, swinging up the trunks of the trees, as if trying to catch the white mushroom snowcaps above.

"It is…beautiful." Mariabella's breath escaped her in a cloud. She stood with Jake on the stone walkway of the Firefly Inn, and felt as if she'd stepped into a Christmas song.

"You like it. I can hear it in your voice."

"I…I love it. I had no idea places like this existed outside of books." She looked up at him. "You own this?"

"Not anymore. My father sold it a few years ago. This used to be what a Lattimore property was like."

"And you changed for…" She waved behind her, in the direction they had traveled.

"For dollars and cents. There's not as much money in little inns tucked away in the country as there is in megahotels in major cities."

"Oh." She drew in a breath, letting the crisp winter air revive her after all the hours in the limousine.

"Do you want to go inside?"

"I thought you did not own it anymore."

"I called in a favor. Come on." He put out his hand.

She slid her palm into his, and even though they were both wearing gloves—his leather, hers wool—she could feel the heat in their touch. Feel the solidity of his large, firm grip. She'd thought today could be just business. A day of nothing but looking at properties and convincing Jake Lattimore why none of his offerings would work in Harborside.

Except she kept forgetting that part of it. And she kept forgetting she was part of the royal Santaro bloodline, and should be acting as such. Using the authoritative mannerisms she had learned to take control of this situation.

But more than that, use the common sense she had learned and stop letting the rest of her body overrule her common sense.

A jingle of bells caught her attention. "What is that?"

Jake glanced at the barn that sat on the right side of the inn. He let out a little laugh. "Can't get any more Christmasy than that."

"What?"

"A sleigh ride." He gestured toward the barn, and then Mariabella saw it. Two horses, attached to a sleigh, like something out of a book or a song.

"I have never seen one in real life."

"Then you've never ridden in one, either?"

"No." She let out a long sigh. "I have always wondered what it would be like. You know, you hear the song on the radio? It sounds so…wonderful. So perfect."

A light dusting of snow had begun to fall, as if Mother Nature wanted to cast the perfect spell over the moment. Jake took her hand and led her down a stone path that led toward the sleigh. "Then let's go."

"Now? I thought we had a schedule to keep."

"The world won't fall apart if the two of us take ten minutes to ride across the snow."

A few minutes later, Mariabella found herself bundled beneath a plaid blanket, seated on a crimson velvet padded seat, while Jake sat beside her, a Thermos of hot chocolate between them. The driver snapped the reins, and the horses started, jerking the sleigh onto the snowy path. The move sent

Mariabella and Jake on a collision course, their torsos meeting, their faces coming within inches. "Sorry," he said.

"Not a problem." She brought the blanket closer to her chin. The faster the horses went, the more winter's cold wind whistled beneath the blanket, her coat, her sweater. She shivered.

Jake put his arm around her, and drew her against his body. Warmth infused her, and so did a heat of a different kind.

She didn't pull away from either.

Instead, she drew the blanket over both of them, and snuggled against him. The horses charged lightly forward, pulling the sleigh through the woods, the bells on their harnesses singing a soft song to match the heavy thudding of their hooves in the snow.

Jake poured her a cup of hot chocolate, and made a joke she laughed at but couldn't remember five seconds later. All she knew was that she was laughing, and he was laughing, and a détente had sprung up between them made all that much sweeter by the cocoa and the snow.

It was, as she'd said earlier, beautiful. And perfect. And so amazingly ordinary.

"Are you having fun?" Jake asked. He brushed his lips against the top of her head, and she leaned closer. Seeking more. Just for now.

"Yes."

"Me, too."

Too soon, the sleigh ride drew to a close, the horses circling back to the barn. Jake helped her down, a smile lingering on his face. "We'll have to do that again sometime."

Did he mean a future with that remark, or was he merely making conversation?

Did it matter, really? When next Christmas came, she'd be in Uccelli. Far from sleigh rides, hot cocoa—

And Jake Lattimore.

"Can we go inside?" Mariabella asked, rubbing her hands up and down her arms. "It is very cold."

"Of course."

Inside, they were greeted by a matronly woman with a wide smile, who told Jake to make himself at home. Several guests filled the downstairs rooms, sitting on the dark brown leather sofas in front of the crackling fire, or in the wingback chairs playing checkers. Others read books by the large picture windows. The scent of apples and cinnamon carried on the air from the kitchen, promising a sweet treat later.

"Let's go upstairs," Jake said. "I want to show you my favorite room in the whole place."

She hesitated, then saw the bright excitement in his gaze, and headed upstairs with Jake Lattimore, even as her better judgment told her being alone with him kept tangling her deeper with a man who awakened a side of her she thought she'd had under control. Yet, every time they were together, she forgot herself. Forgot the objections she had to him.

Forgot her priority—preserving this town.

Every wall in the inn held a photograph, a painting, a piece of memorabilia, that spoke of decades of guests and history. An eclectic mix of furniture, from the rose-patterned wingback chairs to the thick burgundy leather sofa, sent out an air of comfort. Unlike the castle in Uccelli, the charm of this inn existed in its quirkiness, in rooms decorated by chance, not by a professional.

Perhaps this was the key to getting Jake to see how important leaving Harborside alone was to her. If she could equate her town to this place, then maybe he'd understand her fierce love for the town—just as it was—and give up this crazy idea of turning it into a tourist circus. Into the nightmare she had seen in New York.

They went up the first flight of stairs, then turned, headed down the hall and stopped before a small door. Once inside,

Jake flicked on a light switch, then started up another, more narrow flight of stairs. Wood creaked beneath Mariabella's feet, and a slight smell of must and age whispered against her nostrils. She blinked, adjusting her eyes to the dimmer light, provided by a single bulb, then saw where they were.

The attic.

Piles of boxes and sheet-covered furniture pieces filled the space. Cobwebs draped from the corners, and every step they took kicked up a flurry of dust.

"*This* is your favorite room?"

"Not yet." He waved her forward, and she followed, picking her way across the room, dodging crates and stacked chairs, nearly sideswiping a pile of paintings draped with a tarp. A second bare lightbulb sent a harsh stream of light into the room, illuminating a door at the far end of the attic. Jake paused a second, then opened the door, revealing a small, plain room with a twin bed and simple maple dresser. Few decorations accented the space, just a blue braided oval rug, and a pair of white lace curtains hanging like limp soldiers on either side of the lone window.

"You stayed here?" she said. "Why? There are so many rooms downstairs."

"I stayed up here because of that." He pointed out the window, a long, rectangular window that lay so low, one could lie in the bed and stare out at the view all night—a view of the woods, and then, past the forest, the small town nestled at the bottom of the hill. From this distance, the houses and cars seemed to be miniatures, almost doll-sized.

If she hadn't known better, she'd swear she was home in Uccelli. Mariabella moved closer, and rested a knee on the bed. She peered outside, and saw the village below the castle, the people and their homes spread out in a tempting circle around her, a world she could see, but never touch.

The world she longed to be a part of, and couldn't, because of her name. Her station. Her destiny.

She thought of the little boy Jake had once been, who had lain in this bed, and looked out over this view. "You told me you grew up in an apartment in New York," she said.

"I did. A world so different from this one." His voice had softened, dipping into the ranges of memory, of opening a window now to his soul. "But I would come here on vacation once a year with my parents. My father thought I was crazy for wanting this room, but…when I saw this view, and it was just so different from what I had at home, I insisted on staying up here. For a little boy, I guess it was one of those imagination things. Stay up here and dream all day, know what I mean?"

Mariabella nodded, then reached out and touched the pane of glass. "I understand you so much more now."

"You do?"

"We are the same, you and me. At least in what we saw when we looked out the window." She traced the outline of the town below. "From my room, I could see the village below, and at night, when the lights were on, it was like stars had been sprinkled on all the houses. I used to lay there and watch the cars moving, the people walking, then later, after they had all gone inside, I could see them living their lives. Reading by the fire, tucking their kids in at night, laughing with their friends. Just being…normal." She drew in a breath, and looked away from the town. Soon, too soon, she would go back to being the woman in the castle, watching everyone else living the life she wanted for herself. A life she'd only been able to taste, like an appetizer. "It all seemed so…magical from where I was."

Jake had moved to sit behind her on the bed, exchanging warmth. Connection. "Exactly."

Her mind wandered, past the houses below, past the inn, to Uccelli, to the little girl she'd once been, the little girl looking out the window at an impossible dream. "And when the sun came up—"

"It was as if it was coming up just for you. When you're up high like this, the sun seems to be yours alone."

"Yes, it does," she whispered. "It is like you're in your own world. Away from everything that happens below you."

Jake Lattimore understood, she realized, because he had been here, up in this tiny room, just as she had been in her room, at the top of the castle. She could have had any of dozens of bedrooms in the castle, but like Jake, she had chosen the smallest one at the highest point, seeking—

Seeking separation? Seeking distance? Or seeking the best view of the world out there?

"You wanted the same thing, did you not?" She turned around and found herself in his arms. She didn't move back, didn't move away. "The room at the top, so that—"

"I could see what I was missing," he finished.

She swallowed, her gaze connecting with his, wishing, oh, wishing, she had found someone who knew what she had gone through, someone who understood. "And what were you missing?"

His hand came up to cup her jaw. "Freedom."

She closed her eyes. "Yes." The word escaped her on a breath.

"A different life than mine."

"Yes."

And then, his lips were whispering across hers, the heat of his breath caressing her skin. She sank into his arms, and forgot why she shouldn't kiss him—

And just did.

But Jake didn't just kiss her, he awoke a season of feelings in her body, one move at a time. First, with his fingers, dancing along the edge of her jaw, then with his lips, teasing at the edge of hers. She had lived for too long in a winter of nothing, and now she felt as if her body was blooming with emotions, desires, a passion that she had denied, put aside for duty.

For her country.

And yet, Mariabella knew, as wonderful as this was, it had to end. Because it couldn't be, even temporarily. Better to deny herself than have this wonderful thing for a little while, then have it ripped away in two months. She drew back, breaking the contact with Jake, and got to her feet. "That… that should not have happened."

"Because we're at odds over a piece of real estate?"

"That, and because we are from two different worlds."

"It didn't sound so different a minute ago."

She headed for the door, a knife running through her as she remembered she had no right to dream of that life at the bottom of the hill. "We are oceans apart. Further than you will ever know."

CHAPTER SEVEN

THE board had sent out a spy.

Carl Winters leaned against the limo, waiting in the cold. His breath escaped him in a cloud, competing with the smoke coming from the cigar in his hands. A scowl scrunched up his face, darkening his small eyes beneath the black bowler-style hat on his bald head.

"I don't need a keeper." Jake reached past Carl for the door handle.

Carl shifted and blocked Jake's hand. "Seems you do. The board wants action on this deal, and so far, we've got nothing."

"It's Christmas, Carl. People don't make major life decisions four days before Christmas."

"It's your job to make sure they do." He took a step forward. "Your father ran this company into the ground with crazy decisions. That's why we were brought in, to show him how a truly successful corporation is run. He hasn't, however, always listened to our advice, and Lattimore has paid for his…idiocy. We're counting on you to be smarter."

To toe the line, was the unspoken sentence.

"I'm working on it." Jake closed the gap between them, his height giving him a good six-inch advantage over Carl. "Like I told you, I don't need a keeper. I can handle this on my own."

Except, he hadn't done so well with that yesterday, had he?

For a moment there, he'd forgotten business. Actually had the crazy idea of considering the inn, of all properties. What insane sentimental notion had pushed him into driving up there, he didn't know, but he should never have shown it to Mariabella. She needed to understand the more commercially viable property was the one in New York, not a loss leader like the inn.

Given a little more time to make his case, surely he'd show her the downside of those quaint B&Bs she loved, and the benefits of a bustling all-in-one hotel.

Without the distractions of kisses. Definitely no more of those.

"We're just making sure you stick to the plan," Carl said.

As if Jake had any intentions of doing otherwise. He resisted the urge to slam a fist into Carl. "You should remember who is CEO," Jake said, advancing a little on Carl, asserting his authority with his words and height. "I make the plans, and the decisions. I'm the one ultimately in charge of this deal, not you."

"Then stop with the field trips." Carl spun away from Jake, and headed for his car, parked a couple spaces away.

How did the board know where Jake had gone today? No one knew, except Mariabella, Will and his father. He'd told no one else. Jake trusted Will implicitly. Mariabella—

He saw no reason for her to involve the board. That would only go against her goals, rather than work with them.

The only one who could have said anything was Lawrence Lattimore. But why? He was the one who wanted his son to take over as CEO. Unless…

Lawrence doubted Jake's capabilities, too. And had sent out Carl as an insurance policy.

Jake shrugged it off. Until the company was back on solid ground, he'd be proving himself to all the naysayers who thought he'd earned his position through birthright, instead of hard work.

Jake got inside the car, rubbing his hands together to warm them. "There's one guy who's off my Christmas list."

Will laughed. "I saw him coming. Had to resist the urge to push on the gas pedal."

Jake leaned against the seat and ran a hand through his hair. "Maybe I shouldn't work in the family company."

Will stared at him. "You didn't just say that."

"I did. I've been thinking it a lot longer." The empty chasm that had nagged at him for years yawned even wider. Lattimore Properties demanded a type of sacrifice, a compromising of his own ideas and dreams that Jake had accepted when he'd donned the mantle of CEO.

Except, Jake had been wondering lately if he could still make that compromise. Yesterday had only renewed those doubts. Crazy thoughts, yet they kept returning, like boomerangs.

He thought back to the sleigh ride with Mariabella, then the room at the top of the inn. To the blissful happiness he'd seen on her face—and felt in his own chest.

That was the kind of experience he wanted to build. The trouble? Those types of properties didn't make millions. His father and the board would never support such an endeavor. Still…

The empty hole in Jake demanded he fill it with something other than another cookie-cutter hotel. Except cookie cutters sold and sold big.

"Wow. I had no idea," Will said. "I mean, you practically grew up in the company offices."

"Yeah, well, thinking about quitting isn't exactly something I'd bring up at family dinners or at a board meeting."

"Or with your best friend?"

Jake shrugged. "I shouldn't even consider it, that's why I never said anything. My dad is depending on me. Has been for years. I'm his retirement plan." If Jake bucked the company plan, and built a hotel that didn't fit the company model, his father's future would suffer, too.

"Jake, the great savior of the company." Will watched him,

as if trying to gauge his reaction to the words. Will knew Jake better than anyone, knew the expectations that had been heaped on the younger Lattimore for years. "And you have different ideas for your future?"

Jake looked out the window, at the long wooden board-walk lined with shops. A full sidewalk of possibilities for the future of Lattimore Properties, if he did what he was expected to do. "No," Jake said, pulling on the handle and exiting the limo. "I don't."

Carmen had left for lunch, and the gallery had quieted down. The new show would debut tomorrow, the day before Christmas Eve, giving last-minute shoppers both an event to attend and a little something different to buy. All the prepara-tions were done, and Mariabella had turned her attention to her Harborside activities.

She had finished buying the groceries for the annual Christmas Eve dinner she threw for a dozen or so townspeople, and begun the list for the New Year's Eve party at the town hall. She flipped to a clean page in her planner and started working on the wish list for the community center she hoped to have built—or at least started—before she left in February.

So many things to accomplish, and so little time to do them. She'd find a way, though. She'd find a way.

The bell over the door jingled, and Mariabella looked up, expecting a customer. Finding instead Jake Lattimore. Her heart skipped a beat, and her pulse began to race.

She clutched her planner tighter, and refused to let the attraction show on her face.

Ever since that moment in the attic, when he'd kissed her and knocked her completely off-kilter, she'd been unable to concentrate whenever Jake came close. Heck, when she went to sleep last night, she'd dreamed of him, of the laughter they'd shared on the sleigh ride, but most of all, of that kiss.

When she woke up this morning, she'd thought of him. She'd found herself sketching a man with blue eyes in the corner of her planner today.

Insane. She had to shake off these thoughts.

Except a very big part of her didn't want to. That part wanted everything—to find a way to combine duty with the ordinary life she craved like air to breathe.

Jake crossed the room, pausing before the portrait of the mysterious woman. He studied it for a long moment before speaking. "How did you know you wanted to open this gallery?"

The question hit her out of left field. "How did I know? I…I have always loved art. That is what I went to college to study. It is all I have ever known."

More or less. If she left off all that information about the real-life lessons in becoming a queen.

"Yes, but, why a gallery? Why not an art supply store? Or a museum?"

She laughed. "Well a museum is a lot more expensive to own, to stock. To maintain. And, I have been in museums. They are beautiful but not…"

"Not what you wanted." He turned toward her. "Because you had a different vision in mind for your future?"

She thought of the future. There would be no gallery in the days ahead.

Truth be told, she *should* sell Harborside Art Gallery to Jake Lattimore. In a couple of months, she would be leaving for Uccelli, and taking her place beside her father, before finally ascending to the throne.

"No, for my present," she said. Because that was all she had in Harborside.

A slight smile curved up the side of his face, then just as quickly disappeared. "For the present. Of course."

She opened her mouth to tell him she'd given up the fight, she'd sell the shop, then stopped. No. She'd keep the gallery.

Let Carmen run it. She didn't care about making a profit. She simply wanted to know that even if she was on the other side of the world, these days she'd enjoyed wouldn't disappear. It would be like one of those dioramas, something she could peek into with a letter or a phone call, and be transported back to the days when she'd been—

Ordinary.

Jake wandered the room, his gaze roaming over the various pieces of art. He paused by the portrait of the mysterious woman, studying her for a long time, as if he saw the same puzzle in that painting as Mariabella had. "Is this gallery what makes you happy?"

"It…" She paused. "Yes."

He glanced at her. "Why the hesitation?"

"My life is complicated."

He crossed to the window, taking in the view of the ocean. "Complicated. Living here."

She laughed. "Life can be complicated living anywhere."

"True." He spun away from the view and back toward her. The gap between them closed so fast, Mariabella didn't have time to steel herself for his presence, to throw up those defenses she'd worked so hard to convince herself she had in abundance.

"And I have complicated it even more for you," he said.

"Yes. You have."

"Then the best thing to do is to get rid of me."

Her pulse raced, her breath hurried in and out of her chest. She inhaled the woodsy scent of his cologne, and with it, the memory of being in his arms. "It would seem so."

He reached into his jacket pocket and pulled out a sheaf of papers. "This, Miss Romano, is the way to do that."

She stared at him. All this time, she'd thought maybe Jake had come in here to talk about yesterday, about their kiss, about what they had shared on that drive. To tell her that in that room in the inn, he had heard her and now understood her need to preserve Harborside just as it was, because he'd once had the same dreams as her.

Instead, he'd wanted only one thing.

Her gallery.

She swatted the papers away. "I will not sign. Stop asking me."

"Your life is complicated, you told me so yourself. This will make it easier."

"What do *you* know about making my life easier?" She crossed to the desk and flipped open her planner. She dipped her head to study the list of things to do before New Year's Eve. How could she have fallen for that act back at the inn? The romantic sleigh ride? The sweet words?

And that kiss most of all?

Clearly it had all been an attempt to soften her up.

She could read this man like a tabloid. Every time she thought he might be trying to build something on a personal level, might actually be getting to know her—really know Mariabella, the person—Jake Lattimore circled back to what he really wanted. Real estate.

Her cell phone rang, and before she could think about checking the caller ID, she flipped it open, using the call as an excuse to avoid Jake. "Hello?"

"When are you going to end this insanity?"

Her father's voice cut across the phone line with the precision of a knife. Even from the other side of the world, she could hear the disapproval in his tone.

She glanced at Jake, wishing he would leave so she could take the call alone. But he didn't take the hint, and remained in the gallery, a few feet away, yet still close enough to overhear anything she said.

"Are you going to answer me?" None of the sweetness her mother had in his tone.

"How are you feeling?" Mariabella asked, instead of answering the question.

"I'm fine. I'd be better if you were back here. It's been ten months, Mariabella. More than enough time for you to get this craziness out of your system."

She put her back to Jake. "I have until February."

"What difference will two months make? Really, Mariabella, this has gone on long enough. Your place is here, preparing for the throne. Not playing…whatever game you're playing."

"Can we talk about this later?"

"I've sent you an airline ticket by overnight mail. It will arrive tonight, if it hasn't already. I expect to see you here for Christmas. And here to stay."

"But—"

"Your obligations have waited long enough, Mariabella. And so have I." Her father hung up. Discussion over.

Edict issued by His Majesty. No arguments allowed.

Mariabella sighed and tucked her cell phone into her pocket. She would deal with her father later. Somehow.

"Trouble?"

She spun toward Jake and put on a smile. "Everything is fine."

"Good." He slid the papers across the front desk. "About my offer…"

She stared at the purchase and sales he'd put before her. In a few pages, she could sign over the gallery, go back to Uccelli and wash her hands of her life in America. Put it all behind her, dismiss it like a dream she'd once had.

Jake had impeccable timing, she'd give him that. He'd presented her with the way out she needed. The path her father expected her to take.

And take it today.

"What was that yesterday? Who was that man? Because he is not the same one I see today."

Jake scowled. "Forget what I said yesterday. Dreams like that don't make for a successful business."

"And this success you keep talking about, it will make you happy?"

"What does that have to do with anything?"

Mariabella glanced around her gallery, at all that she would soon give up, and relegate to a memory of a time when she had been happy. A man like Jake Lattimore, who had never lived a preordained life of expectations like she had, didn't appreciate what he had. "Happiness fulfills you in a way no amount of money, or privilege, ever can."

He folded the papers into thirds and tucked them inside his jacket. Then he crossed again to the portrait of *She Who Knows*. For a long time, Jake said nothing, then, finally, one quiet sentence. "Have dinner with me."

She hadn't expected that response. "Dinner? With you?"

He pivoted back. "I know there are a hundred reasons why we shouldn't go out again. A hundred more why you probably wouldn't want to see me ever again, especially because I still want to buy your gallery."

"Then why go out at all?"

"Because…" His gaze went past her to the window that looked out over the ocean, to the vast horizon beyond them. "Because my life is complicated, too. And yesterday, when I was with you, it felt a little less complicated for the first time in a long time."

She couldn't say no to honesty like that. Yesterday, she had met a different man. And just maybe, at dinner, she could bring that man back, and persuade him to build the right hotel for this town, before she was forced to meet the demands waiting for her just an ocean away.

CHAPTER EIGHT

"IF YOU don't wipe that smirk off your face, I'll fire you."

The grin widened. Will's smile matched that of the elf's on his blue tie. "Hey, the tie worked, didn't it? You just don't want to admit a bunch of snowmen had more charm than you did."

Jake chuckled. "Okay, so you were right. Half right, anyway. She didn't kiss me. Not that night."

Will arched a brow. "So you *have* kissed her?"

Jake just grinned.

"See? The suggestive power of fun. Give it a day or two and you'll be in love, curled up in front of a fire with her, all cozy for the holidays."

Jake snorted. "It'll take more than that. She's stubborn."

Will glanced at the ceiling. "Like someone else I know?"

"What is this world coming to when the chauffeur is telling the boss what to do?"

"Hey. I prefer the term 'travel director,'" Will said.

Jake laughed again. "Fine. I'll have business cards sent to your office at the front of the limo."

Will's grin had a certain gleam to it, a tease in his gaze, reflected in the rearview mirror. "If you don't mind me saying—"

"You're going to say it either way, so go right ahead."

"—that woman is trouble." Will turned and rested his arm on the back of the leather seat. "Exactly what you need."

Jake scowled. "That's where you're wrong. I don't need any trouble. I need to get this deal done, then get out. I have another property south of San Francisco to look at, then one in Saint Kitts, another in—"

Will mocked a yawn. "Aren't you tired yet?"

"It's six o'clock in the evening, Will. Hardly my bedtime."

"Tired of this grind. Tired of conquering buildings. And going home to…nothing. You don't even have a cat."

"I don't like cats."

"Then get a dog. A goldfish. A parakeet. Something that breathes air into that box you call an apartment."

"Technically, it's a condo. In a building that's netting a fifteen percent return on my—"

Will put up a hand. "Right there. That's the problem. Where do I go on the few days I don't drive you some place?"

"Home."

"Exactly. A real, honest-to-God house. It's nothing much, and I've got a Honey-Do list a mile long, landscaping as overgrown as a rain forest and a dog that my wife walks more than I do, but there's a recliner there with my name on it and a woman who knows exactly how I like my coffee. It's a—" he paused and met Jake's gaze "—home."

"My apartment is a—" Jake stopped. Will was right. The place where Jake put his feet up for a few days a month, the place where he stored his clothes and the books he'd been meaning to read, was a box of walls and windows.

He had once thought he could have a home. Then given up on the idea. Some days he wondered if maybe—

But no. He had a company to run.

Will put out his hands, in a see-what-I-mean gesture. "That's why this woman is trouble."

"Because she has a home?" Jake shook his head. "You

are spending too much time sitting in this car, inhaling carbon monoxide."

His friend let out a sigh, the kind that said his boss had yet to get the point. "Listen, I have no idea if Mariabella Romano lives in a house or a shoebox. What I'm saying is that she's the type of woman who inspires a man to stay home. For a nanosecond, you were that kind of man. And then you became Jake Lattimore, CEO. Apartment guy."

"Then what's the trouble?"

"You're already falling for her." Will turned back around and put the car in gear, pulling away from the curb of the Harborside Inn and heading for the art gallery. The subject closed, but still hanging in the air.

Mariabella stood in the gallery, checking the placement of the paintings for tomorrow night's show, and refusing to check her appearance. Again.

She had already done more than enough primping for an evening that wasn't even a date. It was—

One more opportunity to manipulate Jake Lattimore into leaving Harborside. To convince him he would find bluer waters elsewhere. She had come armed, not just with a dress that showed off her figure—thereby assuring his attention wouldn't wander from her—but also a sheaf of papers in her purse, documenting areas up and down the East Coast that lacked vacation venues.

He wasn't the only one with a few resources up his sleeves.

Except, she fretted, pacing the gallery one more time, dimming the lights for the night as she did, making that call to Reynaldo might have been a mistake. Before, only two people had known her exact location. Now, three did. That multiplied her chances of being found.

Being exposed.

Losing her haven, her serenity.

Mariabella headed into her office, and stopped before a watercolor of a castle. The painting was simple, the lines of the building sparse and stark, but the stone building atop the grassy hill was one very similar to the one where she'd grown up. A local artist had painted it—something the artist had imagined, as a fan of all things fairy tale—and Mariabella had bought the piece for her personal collection because the image was so close, it could have passed for home.

A bone-deep ache bloomed in her chest. She closed her eyes, picturing her parents, wishing she could simply teleport herself back there for one more hug, one more kiss.

Have the best of both worlds. Her freedom, and loving arms.

The bell over the door of the gallery rang, and Mariabella drew herself up. Jake had arrived. And that meant she had to get her game face on, and get down to business. With one last glance at the castle that had been both home and captor, Mariabella strode out of her office and into the main room of the gallery.

She refused to let him know how much he affected her. How she had been thinking, nearly nonstop, about that kiss back in that room in New Jersey.

No. She had to think like a woman in charge, one taking back what was hers—

Harborside.

And that meant using whatever tools she had. She'd learned a long time ago, in dozens of lessons on deportment and protocol, how to make an entrance. She took her time making the walk from the doorway to the center of the room, lengthening her strides, ensuring that the strappy red high heels she wore made her legs look longer, sleeker, beneath the knee-length black dress. Head up, shoulders back, gaze connecting with Jake's.

Commanding the room before she'd even reached him.

His eyes widened, then a smile spread across his face, and

she knew, as she'd known in dozens of state visits and endless balls, that she had his attention. And then some.

"You look…amazing," he said. His voice had dropped into a deeper range, the syllables almost a caress. He took two steps forward, closing the gap between them, and handed her not the traditional chocolates or flowers, but a dozen paintbrushes.

"What is this?"

He smiled. "Carmen told me you paint, too, and I thought this might be a better sign of a truce than a white flag." He pulled a postcard from his jacket pocket and gave it to her. A picture of the inn. "This goes with it."

He'd given her a gift that mattered to her. One that spoke to her passions, and made her remember that day at the inn. Because he was interested in her? Or because he was trying to win her over to his side of the real estate argument by making her think he was on her side, when she knew he wasn't? "Thank you," she said.

"You're welcome." He turned and gestured toward the door. "Are you ready to go?"

She left the gift on the counter, grabbed her coat off the rack, then led the way out of the gallery, locking the shop behind her. Will waited outside the limo, holding the door, a grin on his face. "Good evening, ma'am."

"Hello again, Will." She slid inside the limo. The door shut, sealing Mariabella temporarily in the leather cocoon alone. What was Jake up to tonight? Every time she thought she knew, he reversed course. She found herself wavering between falling for him—and wanting to run him out of town.

Which was the real Jake Lattimore? The one who walked into her gallery that first day, or the one at the inn?

Either way, she knew her only key to getting what this town needed was by appealing to that man she'd glimpsed for a second in the inn. That was the man she had to reach tonight, not the one who had built that New York hotel.

Jake got in on the opposite side, and took the seat across from her. A moment later, the limo pulled away from the curb and began its smooth journey toward the restaurant.

"We could have walked, you know," Mariabella said. "It is only two blocks."

"And it's only about three degrees out. This way, I don't have to worry about you catching pneumonia."

"But then you could take advantage of my weakened state."

He smiled. "Ah, a business strategy I haven't thought of yet. Pump the flu virus into the room, and then bring in the contracts."

"I am sure worse tactics have been employed."

"Not by me." The limo slowed to a stop. "I'm an ethical businessman, regardless of what you might think of me."

She smiled. "I think I will reserve my judgment until after dessert."

He chuckled. "And what if I ask you to go dancing after the crème brûleé?"

"Then poor Will will have an awfully late night, because the closest place for that is Boston."

He leaned forward. "I have all night, Miss Romano, to make my case."

The notes of his cologne carried in the heated air between them. She tried to ignore the dark, woodsy scent, to keep it from affecting her. To keep her gaze from connecting with his cobalt-blue eyes, because in their depths, she saw a heat—

An unmistakable heat, as ancient as the shores that lined the Eastern seaboard. As rocky and treacherous to navigate as the rocky shoals that held Harborside like a north and south cocoon. Desire drew her in, made her forget everything—her goals for this town, her duties back in Uccelli, everything but Jake and how wonderful his kiss had been.

The door opened, ushering in a burst of cold air, and burst of sense. Mariabella jerked back, drawing her coat closed.

Like that put any real distance between them. Still, it was enough to give her mental space, and get her back to reality.

She stepped out of the limousine, thanking Will as she did. "Enjoy your evening, ma'am," he said, then turned to Jake. "Shall I wait, sir?"

"No—" Jake began.

"Yes," Mariabella cut in. "I do not expect us to be out late, Mr. Lattimore. We both have work to do tomorrow, do we not?"

Sending him the clear-cut message with both her words and the use of his last name that this was no date. And he shouldn't expect some endless evening of romance with her.

"As the lady wishes," Jake said, then nodded toward Will, who returned to the driver's side of the limo and pulled it into the parking lot. Jake moved to hold the door for Mariabella, but she had already entered the building herself.

A year ago, she would have waited. Would have expected the man—anyone, really—to treat her in accordance with not just her sex, but her station. Except, after a while, that treatment had grated on her nerves. As if people were treating a title, not a person. Every time Mariabella had tried to do something herself in the castle, she'd been stopped—a princess wouldn't do that; a princess wouldn't behave like that. Since moving to Harborside, Mariabella had enjoyed a sense of self-reliance and strength that went far beyond simply opening her own doors.

She'd opened her own shop. Owned her own home. Mowed her own lawn.

Such simple things, but things she never would have been allowed to do in Uccelli.

"Hi, Mariabella. Table for one? In your usual spot?" Paula, the hostess, asked Mariabella.

"I have a reservation. For Lattimore, table for two, please," Jake said, coming up behind Mariabella and placing a hand lightly on her waist. The familiar gesture, something any date would do, sent a thrill through Mariabella. It was so ordinary, something that wouldn't have happened, had he known she was the princess. There would have been all that stumbling "Your Majesty" stuff in the way.

Paula raised an eyebrow. She stood there for a good three seconds gawking before recovering her hostess manners and managing to look at her reservation book. "Oh, yes, it's right here." She picked up two merlot-colored leatherbound menus. "Uh…right this way please."

"Dine here often?" Jake asked as they made their way toward the dining room.

A hot flush invaded Mariabella's cheeks. She might as well hang a sign around her neck that said Blatantly Single.

"I assume you have a date every night of the week?" she said to Jake. "Some young beautiful woman ready at your beck and call, whenever you jet back to New York?"

"Not quite."

He didn't expound on the answer, and she didn't press. Mariabella got the feeling Jake Lattimore had a few table-for-one evenings in his life, too. Interesting. So she wasn't the only one. Curiosity nudged at her, but she ignored the persistent urge to press him for personal details.

A fire crackled in the wide hearth of the gas log fireplace against the far wall, bathing the room in a soft glow. Pine garland festooned with red bows hung in swags across the mantel, accented with thick vanilla candles sandwiched between pinecones. Wreaths had been hung on the mullioned windows, with electric candles on the sills. The effect was homey and simple, done, Mariabella knew, by the owner herself, complete with all the imperfections that came with homespun décor.

"Can I take your drink order?" Sandy, one of the half-dozen college students who worked at the Captain's Galley in the winter, bounced up to their table, her blond hair back in a ponytail. "The wine list is on the back of the menu."

"Thank you, but I brought along something special of my own. It was an important evening, and I wanted to share my favorite wine with this beautiful lady." Jake flashed Mariabella a smile, then flipped out his cell phone. "Will, could you deliver the 1978 Pinot to the bartender? Thank you."

Sandy headed off, grabbing another waitress on the way, undoubtedly to gossip about the unusual customer who came equipped with his own liquor cabinet.

"You know you will be the talk of the kitchen for days," Mariabella said.

He shrugged. "I'm already the center of a gossip storm. Might as well add to the hurricane." Jake draped an arm over the back of his chair and took in the space. At the same time, the townspeople assessed him, whispers carrying through the room like cold germs in a preschool. "Why do you live in this town?"

"Because I like it here. It is quiet, simple, away from the busy-ness of the city."

"Also what makes it a prime destination spot." He waved toward the windows. Outside, the sun had gone down, and the moon shone a bright white circle above the wreaths. "Harborside has a remote feel without being remote. It's quirky, and yet still maintains some of that uppercrust New England feel. With the right hotel and condos, it can become a mecca for tourists. You have to see the logic in my argument, Mariabella. This idea can work and benefit everyone."

The words grated on Mariabella's senses. "Why are you so set on that idea? Especially after we visited the inn. Something like that would work better, would it not? After all, you loved it so much."

"I do. I did."

She fought the urge to scream at him, to shove him into his limo and drive him out of town herself. "Then why show it to me, if you are still planning on building that other hotel here?"

He put out his hands. "The smart thing for the company to

do is choose the property that will bring in the most return on investment. And while the inn was a nice diversion for the day, it's not smart business."

"The hotel may be the smartest thing to do, but is it the most fulfilling?"

Sandy saved Jake from answering with a glass of his wine, placing one glass before him and another before Mariabella, then leaving the marble carafe holding the bottle beside them. "I'll be back for your order in a minute…unless you have something in your car for dinner, too?"

Jake chuckled. "No, we'll order from the menu."

When Sandy was gone, Mariabella tried her wine. She picked up the glass, lifting the goblet first to her nose, giving the wine a swirl before inhaling the sweet scent, a mixture of citrus with a slight hint of almonds. Then she took a sip. The dry, crisp Pinot slid down her throat smoothly, with a familiar taste.

It couldn't be. That was impossible.

Mariabella took a second sip. But yes, the taste was there. The one she knew. Knew so well.

"Do you like it?" Jake asked. "It's not a common wine, which is part of why I enjoy it so much. Very few people in the States have tasted this one."

She was one of the few who had. She had, in fact, walked the very vineyard that had bottled it. "It is…ah, lovely," Mariabella managed. She put her glass back on the table, careful not to tip it, even as her hands shook.

"I travel quite a bit and sometimes stop off in the tiniest, most out-of-the-way places," he went on, "because I love discovering the best vacation spots. The ones no one else has noticed."

"Really?" The word escaped on a high pitch. Mariabella fought the urge to run. He had to know who she was. He'd done this to set her up.

"Two years ago, I went to Italy, and visited all the normal

spots. Venice, Sicily. I got bored pretty quick, so I decided to go off the beaten path."

Mariabella took another sip of her wine, because she didn't know what to say. Tip her hand now? Or wait until Jake said, *And then I popped into Uccelli and discovered they were missing a princess.*

"So I ditched my driver, rented a car on my own and traveled up the coast." He leaned forward, crossing his arms on the table. His gaze met hers across the small square expanse. "And found the most amazing places."

"Really?" She'd become a one-word parrot.

"Little cafes and shops. Tiny restaurants. Small countries, almost…undiscovered. At least by the corporate lions like me." He let out a laugh.

She tried to join in, but her laughter sounded more like the last-ditch breaths of a strangulation victim.

"My favorite place was this tiny country called Uccelli. Maybe you've been there? Especially where you grew up so close to that area."

What should she say? How much did he know? Panic cut off her air, coiled in her gut. She gripped the stem of the wineglass, so tight, her fingertips turned white.

"So, did you decide?"

Sandy. Thank God. Mariabella could have hugged the waitress for her timing. "I will have…ah…the lobster fra Diablo," Mariabella said. "With a Caesar salad and…and… potatoes au gratin."

Sandy scribbled the order on her pad, then turned to Jake.

"The same."

He'd never even opened his menu. Mariabella had a bad feeling about this dinner. What had really been Jake Lattimore's intentions? Business or pleasure?

In Jake's eyes, she didn't read recognition. He didn't know who she was. His interest in Uccelli was a coincidence, nothing more. Relief settled over her, chased by the warm contentment offered by the wine. Perhaps this evening would turn out better than she had expected after all.

"What did you mean when you said your life is complicated, too?" she asked.

He slid his fork to the side, aligning it with his knife. "You know that sleigh ride we took yesterday?"

She nodded.

"I haven't done anything like that in five years. Like Will told you, I used to be a different man."

"Why?"

His mouth worked, as if he were searching for words. "I haven't had a serious relationship in a long time, and I guess I forgot what it was like to enjoy an evening like that."

"Me, too," she whispered.

He raised his glass toward hers, and they clinked. "To more of that, for both of us."

She didn't respond. She couldn't. How could she tell him her time here was nearly through? That the sleigh ride would become nothing but a bittersweet memory?

Instead, she sipped her wine, and thought of Uccelli, and the fate that waited for her there.

"Is that really what you want?" she asked. "More of that fun?"

"If I can find a way to make it work, yes."

It was time to make her move, to show him there was another answer, another option for his plans. To appeal to the side of him that had reappeared, that side she'd seen yesterday.

She pulled the papers out of her purse and slid them across the table. "Then here are several other possibilities for your hotel. All of them far more suitable for your purposes than Harborside. The populations are slightly larger, which gives your vacationers a wider variety of local businesses, there are more amenities available in a fifty-mile radius—" she pointed to the first one on the pile "—this one even has an outlet mall with two-hundred stores, a big plus—"

"You've put a great deal of time into this in a short period of time." He sifted through the thick sheaf of papers. "I'm impressed."

"I wanted to provide you with options."

"Besides Harborside."

"Yes."

Jake leaned back in his chair and crossed his arms over his chest. "Why are you so hell-bent on driving me out of town?"

"We like our town the way it is. It has all the elements of that inn you loved so much. Why can you not see that?"

"If that's so then why did Louisa Hampton already agree to sell her kite shop?"

Louisa? She had given in? Mariabella had thought Louisa would stand firm, and not sell. She couldn't imagine the boardwalk without the kindly elderly woman and her little dachshund. Every morning, Louisa stopped in at each of her neighbors' shops before opening her own, and said a friendly hello. She had been a staple in Harborside for as long as anyone could remember.

"And my team is already working on contract terms with Sam Carter."

The bike shop owner. Business had been down for him for over a year. The summer rentals just hadn't brought in enough income to sustain him the other three seasons. She could understand Sam wanting to sell, but maybe if she talked to the others—

Then what?

Mariabella couldn't single-handedly save every business in Harborside. No matter how much she might want to.

A second couple came into the dining room and sat down at the table beside them. At first, Mariabella gave them a passing glance—a tall blond man dressed in business casual and a thin brunette woman in a red suit and black high heels.

"If you just consider some of the other—" Mariabella gestured toward the papers, then stopped.

The woman at the next table was whispering to the man with her. And at the same time, staring at Mariabella.

"I will think about these possibilities," Jake was saying. "After this project is completed. Harborside needs something to take it to the next level as a vacation spot, not just for tourists, but for the finances of this town. You must agree with me at least on that. But…perhaps you and I can reach a compromise."

"Compromise?"

The woman was now openly gawking at Mariabella. The attention unnerved her, and she shifted in her seat, trying to keep her attention on Jake. What was he saying? Did he still want to build that monstrosity? Was everything they'd done and said yesterday for nothing?

The woman beside them reached out and touched Jake, drawing his attention. "Hi, Jake."

Jake turned and looked at her. "Darcy. Tim. I didn't expect to see you so soon."

"We rode up with Carl. He thought it would be a good idea for us to check out the town early on in the planning process," Tim, the blond man, said. "Get a feel for what you're envisioning."

Jake gave them one short nod, one that didn't show a trace of emotion, then turned to Mariabella. "Mariabella Romano, this is my team. Tim Collins, my architect. Darcy Singer, my marketing director."

A setup, this whole dinner had been a setup. The wine. The table for two. And now, the "team." The betrayal stung Mariabella and it was all she could do to put on a polite smile.

The two other people put out their hands, as polite as dignitaries at a dinner party. Except…

Darcy kept studying Mariabella. She tipped her head one way, then the other.

Mariabella straightened her spine, and tilted her chin, giving Darcy the slight air of haughty disregard that came with her upbringing. In Uccelli, that look reminded those who might have dared to talk down to the princess that royalty came with certain privileges.

Like respect.

Like not being stared at as if she were a science exhibit.

"A pleasure to meet you," Mariabella said. The words choked out of her. She shot Jake a glare. He started to say something to her, but Darcy interrupted.

"Are you…like, a movie star?" Darcy said. "I swear, I know you from somewhere."

Dread dropped in Mariabella's stomach. She'd seen that look before. Knew that tone.

In the space of one slow second, Mariabella could feel the world she'd worked so hard to build fall apart. Crumbling one syllable at a time.

"Your face is so familiar," Darcy went on. "I know it. Give me a second."

Darcy was on to her. Maybe not all the way, but she was inching closer every second Mariabella stayed.

If she could have run out of the restaurant, she would have. But the wall was behind her, Darcy was in front of her, and Jake was beside her.

Jake stared at her. Waited for her answer to Darcy's question.

"I am afraid you have me confused with someone else," Mariabella said.

"No, I don't think so." Darcy squinted. "I *know* I know you. I read that *Famous People* magazine all the time. It's a vice, I know, and I should be reading business magazines on planes, sorry, Jake," Darcy said, glancing at her boss, "but sometimes you just have to indulge, especially when you spend as much time on planes as I do. And I can swear, I've seen your picture in there."

"I need to go," Mariabella said, getting to her feet. Her stomach rolled and pitched, and sweat broke out on her forehead.

Darcy reached for her, but Mariabella shifted quickly to the right, away from the touch. "I'm right, aren't I? Are you like in hiding or something?"

"You have got me all wrong," Mariabella said.

"I don't think so." Darcy stared at her, and in that second, Mariabella knew she'd met her worst nightmare. "I never forget a face."

CHAPTER NINE

JAKE had wondered who Mariabella Romano was. He'd wondered why she was living in Harborside, and concocted dozens of scenarios in his head, most centering around logical premises. She'd come to America to study, or with a boyfriend.

But he clearly should have been looking to the newsstand for his answers.

Mariabella grabbed her purse and coat and got to her feet. "I really have to go."

In a blur, she was gone.

Without ever answering the question.

"Well, that was weird," Tim said.

"I agree." Jake tugged the wine bottle out of the carafe and poured himself a second glass of the Pinot. He was about to put the bottle back into the holder when Darcy stopped him.

"Hey, let me see that." She turned the bottle around, studying the design on the front. "I've seen this painting before." She thought a second. "I know. In the same magazine. They did this whole article on this little country north of Italy, how it was like one of the last monarchies in the world, and—"

She stopped talking.

Stared at Jake, then at where Mariabella had gone.

"That's impossible," she whispered.

"What is?"

Darcy cradled the bottle, running her thumb over the image. "I can't believe it."

"What?"

Darcy handed the bottle over to Jake and pointed at the label. The front had, as Darcy had said, a painting. A stone castle, the same one he'd seen on his brief visit to Uccelli, rising above the rocky shore and lush green paths. It was as he'd remembered, with four turrets topped with purple and gold pennants, surrounded by a massive stone wall, that he imagined had once been manned full-time by guards.

He spun the bottle around to read the back. "'Grown and bottled at a vineyard located just down the hill from the royal palace, an impressive stone structure built in the late seventeenth century. A small but thriving country, Uccelli is one of the few remaining monarchies in Europe.'"

"Monarchy? As in kings and queens?" Tim said.

"That's the place." Darcy pointed to the image on the bottle. "That's the castle I saw in the article."

"And what does this have to do with Mariabella?"

"She was…" Darcy leaned forward, her eyes wide with excitement. "The *princess*."

Jake scoffed and put the bottle back in the carafe. "Come on. There's no way a princess is living in this little town. And no one knows about it."

Darcy shrugged. "Maybe. Or maybe not. It happens."

"With who? Cinderella?"

Tim chuckled.

"I could be wrong." But as Darcy said the words, Jake got the feeling she doubted she had made a mistake, and knowing his efficient marketing director as he did, he doubted it, too. "Either way, I'll be glad to research it."

Jake gave a single nod. As quickly as Mariabella had left, he sent Darcy and Tim off to research and told them he would have their meals delivered to the Seaside Inn.

That pushed his team off on another mission besides watching his every move, which was undoubtedly what Carl had brought them here to do. To ensure Jake fulfilled the board's orders, got the signatures on the real estate transactions and built a shining example of a Lattimore property. None of those silly sentimental buildings his father had once loved.

He waved over the waitress and paid the bill. For now, the real estate transaction would wait. He had a more important mission of his own to accomplish.

"She doesn't exist," Tim said.

"What do you mean, she doesn't exist?" Jake barked into his cell phone, then lowered his voice and apologized. "There has to be an address, a phone number, something for her. No one lives in this country for almost a year without leaving some kind of paper trail."

"Apparently, she does. And as for Uccelli, all official pictures of her have been taken down. I couldn't find a single one on the Internet. It's like she…vanished."

Jake paced outside the limo, his breath escaping in a cloud. A melody, followed by the rise and fall of laughter, caught his attention. People streamed in and out of the Clamshell Tavern, a few humming along with the Christmas carol playing inside. "She may not have left a paper trail, but I bet she left a people trail." Jake told Tim to keep trying to dig up information, then hung up, gave Will a sign to wait and jogged across the street.

As he'd expected, he found Zeke sitting at the same stool, only this time the tavern was far more crowded, with several people playing pool, a few dancing around the jukebox and a group of men cheering on a hockey team on the big screen at the opposite end of the bar. Jake slid in beside Zeke, and ordered the man a beer. "Hey, Zeke."

"Hey, Mr. Lattimore. You still in town?"

"I'm here until the job is done."

Zeke grinned. "Hard-working man. That's something I can respect. 'Course, can't say I can relate, but I can respect it." He tipped the beer bottle Jake's way. "You working at night?"

Jake was about to say yes, then shook his head. "Thought I'd just have a beer right now." He ordered a second bottle for himself, and settled into a relaxed pose. As if he had all night.

"What do you think of them?" Zeke said.

It took a second before Jake realized the man meant the hockey team battling it out on the television screen. "I like them if you do."

Zeke chuckled. "I do, but I don't say that too loud 'round these parts. You gotta root for the home team, know what I mean?"

"I do."

Jake thought of the season tickets to the basketball team that sat on his desk, year after year, used more often by his assistants than by him. Same with the box seats to baseball. For a second he watched the crowd around him, regular working men and women, who roared at each turn in the action.

And he envied them.

They took the time to go to bars and games, to have lives like Will's. Maybe his friend was right. Maybe it was time to put work aside and live, like he had yesterday.

Except yesterday had been spent with a woman who had been lying to him, who had been hiding a secret the entire time she'd been in his arms. Maybe it was better to stick to work. At least a profit and loss was always written in black and white.

The period ended, and a commercial came on, causing the crowd around the television to break into small groups doing a verbal rehash of the last few moments of play, along with resounding criticism of the refs and the coaches.

"Ah, they're losing." Zeke frowned and turned away. "I know how it's going to end. Badly."

"Then why do you watch?"

Zeke's frown turned into a grin. "Because at heart, I'm one

of those sappy guys who believes in happily ever after. Just don't tell the ladies, or they'll be expecting me to go around with flowers and wine." He puffed out his chest. "Gotta protect my image as a tough guy, you know."

Jake chuckled. "Your secret's safe with me." He toyed with the beer bottle. "Speaking of women, I took Mariabella Romano to dinner tonight."

He didn't add how it had turned out, that he had realized she was leading a double life. From the look on Mariabella's face earlier, Jake doubted anyone in town knew the truth about her.

Zeke's jaw dropped. "And she went? On a date?"

"You're surprised?"

"Our Mariabella doesn't date much," Zeke said, then thought a second. "Actually, I've *never* seen her date."

That would make sense for someone protecting their identity. The question was why. And why she was so fiercely protective of a little town on the other side of the world.

"Things ended badly," Jake said. "And I was hoping to make it up to her."

Zeke gave him a little nudge in the ribs. "A secret flowers-and-wine counterattack? Is that it?"

"Exactly." The one-word lie slid off Jake's tongue easily. But it tasted bitter.

He didn't know why it should. After all, she'd been lying to him from day one. He'd opened up to her and where had it gotten him?

Nowhere but distracted from the plans he should be focusing on. From here on out, things between them would be business, pure and simple. He had no intentions of wooing Mariabella Romano for anything other than her location. And that meant using every tool at his disposal.

Including her identity.

"Our Mariabella might not be the wine-and-roses type."

Zeke rubbed at his beard. "You're going to have to work a little harder, my boy."

"You keep calling her 'our Mariabella.' Is there a reason why?"

Zeke shrugged. "This town unofficially adopted her when she moved here. We took care of her, and she's taken care of us."

"Financially."

"Hell, no. Though what she did for us has brought us up in the dollars-and-cents department. She's started committees, arranged events, just got us organized and thinking in new ways. She's been a real leader 'round here." Zeke took a deep drag from the beer, then put it back on the bar. "Anyway, it ain't none of my business to be talking about her behind her back. You want to know about Mariabella, you have to do your own homework."

He had Tim and Darcy doing some of that homework. The type that could be done on computers, with background checks and phone calls. What Jake wanted to do involved a more…personal connection. "I'd like to get to know her better," he said, "but she's a tough nut to crack."

Zeke chuckled. "She is stubborn, I'll give you that."

"I do feel bad about how things ended tonight," he repeated, hoping to work on Zeke's sympathies, "and if I knew where she lived, perhaps I could tell her in person. If I wait until tomorrow, she'll be so busy at the gallery, that I may miss my chance."

Zeke shifted on the bar stool. "I don't think Mariabella would like me to give out her address."

"You're probably right." Jake signaled for another round. The bartender slid two more beers their way. "Waiting until tomorrow to apologize for spilling a drink on her new dress probably won't hurt…."

"Oh, boy, that's a bad one!" Zeke crowed. "I did that once

to my first wife, and I was in the dog house for a week! Cost me not one, but two new dresses."

Jake nodded, and studied his beer. "I suspect I'll be paying. For quite some time. But I suppose I can make it up to her later. Maybe."

"First date you say, huh?"

He nodded again.

"I know a lot of us around here sure would like to see Mariabella with a fellow." Zeke stroked his beard. "And you seem like a nice enough man."

"My fifth grade teacher will vouch for me." He gave Zeke a grin, one he hoped built camaraderie.

Zeke grabbed a pen from the bar, then scribbled something on a cocktail napkin and slid it over to Jake. "You didn't get that from me. But if this works out, I want to be front and center for the wedding."

Jake's smile wobbled on his face. Wedding? That was as far from his plans as Pluto was from Earth. "You've got it, Zeke."

He left the Clamshell Tavern, leaving behind a promise he didn't mean, made to a man he hardly knew. It was business, he told himself.

Then why did something he did every day suddenly feel so wrong?

"He wants me on the next plane home," Mariabella said. The plane ticket sat on the table before her, bright red and white.

Demanding.

She tucked herself into the chair, the plaid wool afghan drawn tight around her legs, but it didn't block the stress whispering at her nerve endings. She'd come home from the restaurant, terrified that Jake would come running up her walk, announcing he'd recognized her. Calling out her real name. Calling her *Princess*.

He hadn't, so in that area, she was still safe.

Maybe Darcy had gotten her confused with some soap opera star or someone else and the whole incident would blow over. The churning worry in Mariabella's gut said otherwise.

She'd come home tonight to an overnight delivery truck in the driveway, a driver waiting with a pen in his hand and an envelope with her name on it. Her father had done as he'd promised, and sent the ticket. For a few hours today, she'd hoped maybe her father had been bluffing.

She knew better. Franco Santaro never bluffed. Never joked. He ordered—and he got what he ordered.

"I know what your father has said." Her mother let out a long breath. "He is insistent this time. But, I will talk to him. Tell him two months will make no difference."

"You know how he gets, Mama. He won't listen."

"He will. He did the first time."

But her mother's voice lacked conviction, and Mariabella knew the chances of her father changing his mind had dropped from zero to a negative number. The king had made up his mind—and he expected to see his daughter at Christmas dinner in three days.

"I'll come home on the next plane," Mariabella said. "It will make him happy and be easier for—"

"No!" The word escaped her mother in a forceful shout. "Stay where you are until your birthday."

"Mama…"

"No. Once you come back, you will be trapped in this life forever. You know it, I know it. Take this gift of freedom while you have it. I will talk to him, and remind him of his agreement." Her mother paused. "Find your heart, my daughter. You may never have another chance."

"I already did find everything I wanted, Mama," Mariabella said, even though the thought giving up all of that made something shatter inside her. "My gallery is a success—"

"Have you found love yet?"

"I didn't come here for love."

Her mother tsk-tsked. "The right man could be anywhere."

Mariabella laughed. "Mama, I'm not ready to get married. I don't want to get married. I'm happy as I am."

"Are you?"

Two words, a simple question, and yet they hit a nerve both women knew ran deep. Mariabella Santaro had led a solitary life, much like the Rapunzel of fairy tales, stuck in the castle, not by an ogre or an evil prince, but by duty. By honor.

For Mariabella, dating had always been a disaster. Men made too nervous by her position, or too ambitious by her last name. She hadn't met a single one who had seen her as just Mariabella.

Her mother, bless her heart, didn't understand. Franco Santaro had married a woman outside the monarchy, a woman who had not grown up in that steel bubble of judgment. Bianca had been a member of the aristocracy, an approved bride, chosen by his parents, so she would be acceptable, both to the crown and to the populace. Despite the odd beginnings of their marriage, Bianca had fallen in love with her husband, and had been happy for decades.

Mariabella hoped some day to find that kind of happiness, but she had yet to find a man who could see past the crown she would someday wear.

She thought she had, but—

Tonight that had all likely been ruined.

"You need to settle down, Mariabella. You're getting older," her mother said. "Promise me, you'll open your heart, too, while you are in America. And give some man a chance."

Mariabella sighed. "I'll…try."

The image of Jake Lattimore sprang to mind. His deep blue eyes, the way they seemed to pierce through the thick armor she'd built around her true heart. So many times, he'd gotten so close to her, close enough that she could have slipped and nearly told him everything.

If she had, would he have looked at her the same way? Held her, kissed her, the same? Or would he have run from the pressures of being with a royal?

Maybe he had put the pieces together tonight and that was why he hadn't come to her house. Maybe he'd decided a princess carried too much baggage for an ordinary man to handle.

This was why she didn't open her heart. Why she didn't give men a chance. Because once she did, and they knew who she really was, they stopped seeing her as a woman and instead saw her as an object, a crown on a pedestal.

How she wanted to be seen for herself, to have someone look past the exterior and look inside.

"You know the one thing that will change your father's mood," her mother was saying, "and bring back the smiling man we all remember?"

Mariabella tried to think of who her mother meant, because as far as she could think back, her father had always been the monarch, stern and judgmental. "What?"

"Grandchildren."

Mariabella scoffed. "Mama, I'm not even dating anyone. Don't talk about children, too."

Her mother laughed. "If you need someone to date, your father is talking about Ricardo Carlotti again."

Mariabella scowled. "Mama, I don't even like him. He's...dull. Predictable as a cloud. Spends more times reading than he does looking at me. He'd be happier marrying a library."

"Your father thinks he'd make a good match. And," she continued before Mariabella could interject, "your father would like to see you married before you ascend to the throne."

"I don't want to get married. Or ascend."

Her mother was silent. The former might be an optional choice, but the latter was a foregone conclusion. She was the firstborn of three daughters.

The plane ticket glared at her. Waiting patiently, but with one clear message.

Go home.

"Bella, I did not grow up a royal," her mother said, as if reading her daughter's mind, "but because of that, I know what it is like to live an ordinary life. I also know what it is like to become queen, and to see your father's life as king. I have lived both sides of the coin, and understand your frustrations, your desires. As a princess, you had more freedoms than you'll have as the monarch, even if it didn't feel like you did."

"I know." She hadn't had the multitude of state duties, the dinners, the meetings that consumed her father's days. She'd had the expectations of decorum and a number of events, but nowhere near the total her father attended.

"I want you to live the life I had, for as long as you can, before you're…laced into the corset of that crown. Don't get on that plane. Your father can wait two months."

"He won't be happy."

"I know," her mother said quietly.

"He's…" Mariabella paused. "He's never been happy with me."

"He loves you, *cara.*"

"That's not the same thing, not when I've never felt loved by him."

There. The words were out. They weren't all of them, but they were a large part of what she had been feeling for so many years. For a long time, her mother didn't say anything, and all Mariabella heard was the crashing of the waves outside her cottage, the hum of the phone line.

"He's a difficult man. A stubborn one."

"That does not give him an excuse, Mama."

Her mother let out a long breath. "No, it doesn't. I think…he is too much of a king. He forgets to be a father."

"If that is the kind of queen I will end up being...I don't want to wear the crown."

"I understand. But you won't be like him. You'll be yourself, Mariabella."

Mariabella glanced out the window, at the country, and the town, she had come to love, because it was here that she had finally become herself. Neither her father nor her mother seemed to understand that. They saw only duty, not Mariabella's heart.

"I'll try, Mama," she said, the words escaping on a sob. She tried to call the tears back, but they pushed past her reserves, fell down her cheeks and dropped onto the only course of action Mariabella had.

The plane ticket home.

Mariabella said goodbye to her mother. She had no other options left. She had better face that now, before she got any more attached to this place.

She rose, crossing the living room, her bare feet padding across the hardwood floors, then meeting the cool tile of the kitchen.

A small house, a cottage really, nothing much by most people's standards. But it sat on the edge of beach, and was kissed by the salty air each morning. The cottage held none of the grandeur or servants of the castle, but Mariabella didn't mind. She loved every inch of the wood frame, the wide pine floors and the white wicker furniture she'd bought herself.

The doorbell rang. Probably Carmen, here to plead her case again about getting Mariabella to hang some of her own paintings in the gallery. Mariabella swiped the tears off her face, then opened the door, expecting a friend.

And got instead Jake Lattimore, with a bouquet of flowers, another bottle of wine and a smile. Not the person she wanted to see, not now, not after the conversation she'd just had. And not after what had happened in the restaurant.

Then she thought of the time in that room in the inn, how he'd looked out over that small town, and seen something similar to what she had seen every day of her childhood. Perhaps he could understand what she felt right now, and realize why she had lied. Perhaps leaning on him could ease the ache in her heart brought on by the thought of leaving.

"May I come in?"

She debated saying no, knew she should say no. She didn't need to entangle herself in a personal relationship, especially not now. She was leaving, probably in the morning. Her moments of normalcy were over. No sense dragging this out another minute. But oh, how she needed someone's shoulders to lean on, someone to hold her and tell her everything would be fine.

Someone who would make her forget for just a minute, when he whispered her name. Touched her. Kissed her.

"I promise, I only want to talk to you." Jake extended the flowers forward. "And to say I'm sorry for tonight."

The fresh scent of white Gerbera daisies, accented with red roses, green kermit poms and holly berries, teased at her senses. An unexpected surge of joy rose inside her. She'd received flowers before—by the truckload, from enraptured suitors determined to win her heart. Once, two wealthy men from Uccelli had gone head to head in their battle to convince Mariabella to go to the annual ball with them. They'd played one-upmanship with flowers, sending so many, the florists in the city had finally begged Mariabella to end the war because they couldn't keep up with the demand.

She'd opted to go alone, and given each man equal time on the dance floor. And donated all of the flowers to the hospital and nursing home.

But these—these were chosen just for her. They were beautiful in their simplicity. "Thank you."

"I apologize for my team being at the restaurant tonight. I had no idea they were coming to town."

Get rid of him. He already knew she wasn't who she said she was. A day, maybe two, and he'd figure out who she was. If it took even that long. Then he would bring in the media, and the frenzy would disrupt the peace in Harborside. Her friends, her neighbors, would be upended by the constant barrage of questions and intrusions into their lives. Not only would the fabric of the town be destroyed by the Lattimore resort, but the tranquility would also be erased simply because of her presence.

Don't let the flowers sway you. Or his words. Or his smile.

"Jake, I'm sorry, but this isn't a good time," she said. "And after tonight—"

His gaze lit on the space behind her. "Wow. You surprise me."

"What are you talking about?"

"I thought you'd be more of a portrait artist. Maybe landscapes. But these…" A smile took over his face. "Amazing."

Mariabella followed his gaze. Her pulse skittered to a stop. Oh, no. Her paintings. He'd seen her paintings.

Suddenly, she felt naked, exposed, as if she'd gotten on a stage and started reading from her diary. She wanted to rush over to the artwork and throw a cloth over the paintings, hide them from his inquisitive view.

"May I?" Jake asked, gesturing toward the art stacked against the far wall.

If letting him into her home was like giving him access to her identity, letting him see her art was like giving him access to her soul. She shouldn't. She hadn't let anyone see her art, except for Carmen, who'd merely had a glimpse when she'd stopped by one time.

And yet, even as everything within her said no, she found her mouth saying "yes."

It had to be the flowers. In the palace, there'd been fresh flowers every week, sometimes every day for special occasions. But none of them had been chosen especially for her.

None of them had been hand-delivered by a man with an apology. And a smile like that.

"First, tell me something."

He cocked his head and studied her. "Okay. What?"

"Why did you bring me a bouquet?"

"Uh…because women like flowers." He rubbed his temple. "Is this a trick question?"

"Why one bouquet? You are a wealthy man and…" She searched for the right words, ones that wouldn't offend him, and yet would say what she needed to say.

"A man who could buy an entire flower shop, if I needed to?"

She nodded.

"I thought of that," he admitted. "But then I realized you weren't that kind of woman."

"What made you realize that?"

He took a step closer to her, and her heart began to race. She drew in the scent of his cologne, and with it, the sense of danger that came with getting any closer to this man. To getting closer to anyone. "Back at the inn, I saw another side of you."

He had listened after all. Of all the people who had known her, all the people in her life, this man, this near stranger, had paid attention. Even her mother, who loved her, didn't know her heart the same way. Finally, a man who saw her as a woman, a person, not a princess.

Too bad he was too late.

"What did you see?" she asked, knowing she shouldn't wrap herself in him anymore, but unable to resist.

He caught a tendril of her hair, and let the silky tress slide through his grasp. Her breath lodged in her throat, every ounce of her stilled, waiting. "I saw a woman who has watched the world from a tower, and never got to live in it until she moved here."

Mariabella nodded. "And you, did you ever get to live in the world you watched?"

He shifted away from her, and crossed to the artwork. The conversation had ended as quickly as it had started. One door opened, another slammed shut. "What technique is that?" he asked, bending down to study the work closer. "It looks three-dimensional."

She should be happy. After all, didn't she want to keep things on an impersonal level? Maintain that distance from a relationship, especially for the limited time she had left in America?

Curiosity nudged at her, pushing her closer to him, even as her better judgment told her to back away. "You have asked me a lot of questions. And have told me almost nothing about you," she said. "Who are you, Jake Lattimore?"

"There's not much to know. I work." He grinned. "And I work."

"And watch the world go by instead of getting involved with someone?"

He looked away. She waited, refusing to fill the silence. Time ticked by, seconds marked by the crashing of the waves outside the tiny cottage. Jake crossed to the mantel and fiddled with a ceramic Santa. "There was someone. Once," he said finally.

"What happened?"

He swallowed. The firelight danced across his face, casting the depths of his face into shadows. "She died a month before our wedding. Car accident."

"Oh, Jake, I am so sorry." She went to him, her hands lighting on his back, but he didn't turn around. He held the grief inside him, in a deep place she couldn't reach, couldn't ease for him.

"I never thought—" He heaved a breath. "I never thought I'd get over it."

She leaned her head against the soft fabric of his shirt. The fireplace warmed him from the front, she from the back, but Mariabella knew there was still an ice inside of Jake Lattimore that had yet to thaw.

"And so I worked. It was easier to do that than to live."

"You have been in a prison," she said softly, understanding him so much better now, a man who was a kindred spirit to hers, but for different reasons, "for all these years."

He turned around in her arms. "Yeah, I guess I have."

How she wanted to tell him that she would be here, if he ever decided he was ready to have another life. To move forward. But how could she make that promise? How could she give him a gift she didn't even have?

Across the room, the plane ticket waited. And across the world, her father waited.

"Someday, you will find someone—" the words hurt her mouth as she said them "—and I am sure you will be very happy."

Something flickered in his gaze, something that turned the warmth in his blue eyes cold. "Yeah. Someday."

She broke away from him. She wanted to comfort him more, but she couldn't touch Jake for one more second and fool herself into thinking she didn't care about him.

Because she did.

And forgetting him was already going to be a Herculean task.

He seemed to be thinking the same thing, because he returned to the stack of paintings. "How do you make these 3-D?" His voice had gone distant.

He'd already drawn away from her, too.

She should have been relieved by the change in subject, but a part of her felt disappointment. She brushed off the feeling and focused on her art. "It is called relief painting. I use industrial resin on wood fiber board, to shape the figures, and then I paint the details with oil paints." There. Talk about techniques on canvas.

"They look so real. This one…" He paused. "Incredible."

The one he'd chosen had been one of Mariabella's personal favorites. Two pelicans, diving into the ocean, racing to catch a fish both had spied from the air.

"It was a moment I saw one day, back in the summer, and I wanted to capture that competition, that air war."

"You brought them to life," he said. "The three dimensions make them seem vibrant, so real, and the colors you chose…wow. The way you painted the sun breaking on the horizon behind the birds, it's as if I'm there, standing on the beach."

Heat filled her cheeks. She'd had her work critiqued in college, of course, but never had she had such overt praise heaped on one of her paintings. "Thank you."

"You're incredible, Mariabella." He took her hand, then tugged her over to him, into his arms. She fit perfectly, as if she'd always been made for that space against his chest. Oh, this was trouble. Big trouble.

She was falling for Jake Lattimore. And falling hard. No matter how hard she tried not to, to remind herself she was leaving, that she had to put him in the past now, before it got too hard later, she fell even more.

He looked down at her and smiled, and everything about his face softened, drew her in, captivated her even more. "I lied to you."

"Lied?"

He traced the outline of her jaw, and Mariabella nearly came undone with desire. "When I arrived at the gallery, I lied. I said I wasn't looking for anything for my office. But now I realize I am."

His gaze drifted toward the painting of the pelicans, and she connected the dots. "Oh, no, that is not for sale. It is not ready, I cannot…no."

"If you don't want to sell that one, I'm sure I can find another one I like just as well." Jake released her to flip that painting forward, revealing one with a trio of geese in flight, their wings spread broad, the horizon ahead of them—their new destination blurred—and a rocky, barren landscape to the rear. "Like this."

"I cannot sell that one, either. Or any of my work."

"Why not?"

"I…I just cannot."

"Surely you didn't paint all these just to leave them against the wall?"

"I am just not comfortable with having my work out in the public eye."

"What about my eye? Just mine?"

What was he saying? Did he want something more, something just between them?

Oh, how she did.

But she couldn't have that. Jake Lattimore was like the toy in the window a child wanted for Christmas and the mother couldn't afford. He would always be behind the glass of another world. She had a duty to fulfill, and no matter how much she wished otherwise, he wasn't part of that duty. An ache spread through her chest, her veins. "I cannot let it go," she said, meaning everything but her art. "I am…I am sorry."

I cannot let you go.

I cannot leave.

His gaze met hers, and held for a long moment. "Me, too," he said. "I would have loved to have this."

Did he mean the painting? Or her? Better not to know. Easier.

She didn't answer him. He went back to flipping through the paintings. "Why birds?"

"I like birds." There was more to the answer than that. But telling him the rest involved telling him where she came from, about her quest for freedom, about the constant itch to be anywhere but back in Uccelli.

About the fight in her heart between duty and her own life, as if she were a wild bird caught in a manmade cage.

"Me, too." Jake got to his feet and met her gaze with his own. The quiet of her house, which seemed so peaceful when it was just her, seemed to boil up with tension. "Especially yours."

"Thank you." Heat rose in her cheeks, and she dipped her gaze. When he stared at her like that, the intensity took her to places she hadn't visited before. Opened doors she had always kept shut. Asked her questions she'd never answered.

Could she fall in love? Could she have a life with a commoner?

She didn't ask those questions because she knew the answers. A commoner, particularly an American businessman, would never be acceptable to her father. To the kingdom.

"Why aren't these in your gallery?" Jake asked.

"I am hosting another artist right now." Not a lie, entirely.

"You should host you." His gaze swept over her face. "But if you do, there would be publicity and that would let people know you are…?" He arched a brow.

"I better put those flowers into water before they die." Damn. That's what she got for inviting him in. He circled back around to the one subject she wanted to avoid.

Who she was.

Mariabella hurried into the kitchen. She looked for a vase, then realized she didn't have one. She'd never had a need for one before. She pulled a pitcher out of the cabinet, filled it with water and arranged the bouquet in the glass container, using the ribbon from the package to accent the handle.

"Darcy has this crazy idea," Jake said.

At some point, he had followed her into the kitchen and was leaning against the wall. Mariabella froze at the words. Darcy. That woman who had almost recognized her. Did she know? Had she figured it out after Mariabella left the restaurant?

Impossible. Wasn't it?

"Oh…yeah?" She fiddled with the flowers.

"She thinks you might be a princess."

Mariabella swallowed hard. She plucked out a daisy from the center and shoved into a space on the side, then moved a rose from the right to the left. "Huh. Really?"

"Are you?"

The two words hung in her kitchen, heavy, fat with anticipation. Destructive.

Are you her?

Mariabella planted her hands on either side of the counter. What should she do? Lie and hope he didn't uncover the truth? Or tell him yes, and sit back, wait for the media onslaught that would destroy everything she had worked so hard to build?

Jake Lattimore was a man of means. And those means would lead to the answers he sought, one way or another.

It was over. Her life here. Her fantasy that she could be loved by a man like him, as an ordinary woman. Once she told him who she was, he would never look at her the same way again.

Mariabella closed her eyes and in her mind, said goodbye to a relationship that had never really had a chance to begin. She straightened her back and turned to face him. When she did, her body naturally rose into its perfect alignment, the balance-a-book-on-your-head posture she had learned so long ago. She drew in a deep breath, then released it. "I am, indeed, Princess Mariabella Santaro of Uccelli." She paused, then met his gaze. "But if you tell anyone, I will make sure you never build another hotel in this country or any other."

He had been so sure Darcy was wrong.

But no, here he was, standing in the middle of a tiny cottage in Harborside, Massachusetts, with the heir to the throne of Uccelli. A woman who seemed as ordinary as any other, who could have just come home from buying groceries—and maybe had.

The admission explained everything. Her accent, the way she carried herself, her reluctance to tell him anything about herself. And most of all, the nagging sense he'd had that she was *different*.

He'd never expected *this* kind of different, though.

A princess.

A future queen?

"You are staring at me," she said. "I hate that." Mariabella turned away and crossed to the kitchen cabinets and opened one of the wooden doors, exposing a neatly stacked set of white dishes. She stood there, as if she didn't know what she wanted or why she'd opened the door.

"I'm sorry," he said. "I've just never met a princess before."

"I was a princess when you met me."

"I didn't know you were a princess then."

She pivoted back. "So this makes things different? You see me now as someone else? Someone you should bow to or some such ridiculous thing? Or maybe a curiosity? Like a monkey in a zoo?"

"No. I just…" He took a step closer. "I wonder why you lied to me."

She threw up her hands. "Is it not obvious? I am trying to live my life here as a person, not as a princess. I do not want the media glued to my back, taking a photograph of everything I do, being there when I go into the coffee shop and order an espresso, or go to the grocery and pick up basil. I want to be like everyone else."

"You can do that and still be honest with the people around you." No hurt invaded him, simply a need to understand. He could see how the whole princess thing might have been hard to bring up in a conversation, but still wondered why she had chosen this life of anonymity when she held so much more sway as Princess Mariabella.

She let out a gust. "You think it is so easy? You think I can just say, good morning, I am a princess, but treat me like I am just like you, and that easily—" she snapped her fingers "—it will happen?"

He winnowed the gap even more. "How do you know if you don't give people a chance?"

"People...like you?"

He could easily say no. Mention anyone in town. Cletus. Zeke. The caterer, Savannah, or even Mariabella's assistant, Carmen. Those people had known Mariabella the longest, known her as Mariabella Romano, and never had an inkling that all this time they'd had a real-life princess living among them.

But he'd be lying if he did. From the minute he'd met her, and they'd tangled over the property, over this town, Jake had been intrigued. His senses had been awakened, in a way he'd never thought possible again. For so long, he'd thought his life would never again have that spark, that need for another person.

Until now. Until Mariabella.

"Yeah, people like me," he said quietly, and reached up, to cup her jaw. He lowered his head, his mouth hovering over hers.

She inhaled, and her eyes widened, the light crimson color in her cheeks rising. As tempting as the fabled apple.

The tension between them coiled tighter. Jake gripped her waist, and brought her torso to his. Desire thundered in his head, pulsed through his veins. He didn't see a princess. He didn't see a gallery owner. He saw Mariabella, a woman who made him feel alive for the first time in years.

A woman he had begun to care about. A lot.

And that was the woman he kissed.

When his lips met hers, sensations exploded at every place they touched. She was sweet in his arms, then hot, as she curved against him, and her hands ranged up his back to draw him even closer. His hands tangled in her long, thick dark curls.

Outside, the winter storm kicked up, wind battering the little house, shaking the timbers and whistling under the roof, but it was nothing compared to the storm brewing between Jake and Mariabella. This kiss wasn't like their first one. It wasn't short, it wasn't sweet, it was a storm, like the one outside.

The tumult in their kiss reached a feverish pitch, and they each took a step back, until she was pressed against the counter, and his length was pressed against hers, bodies molding into one, their tongues dancing together, mimicking what their bodies could do. Fire roared through his veins, blinding his thoughts to everything but this. His hands snaked up and ranged over her waist, then her breasts, cupping the generous fullness through the soft fabric of her sweater. Mariabella arched against him, and let out a soft moan. Jake nearly fell apart, and the fire in him reached a level that would not be easily quieted.

Suddenly, she broke away, and stepped over to the sink, her back to him. "What…what are you doing?"

His breath came in heaves, his mind a jumble. "I thought I was kissing you." And he'd thought she'd been responding. Had he misread everything? The invitation in her eyes? The answer in her lips to the question posed by his own?

"Kissing *me?*" she asked, still not facing him, her voice quiet. "Or kissing a princess?"

"Is that what you think this was? I find out who you are, rush right over and grab you, so I can run out and tell the tabloids I kissed a princess?"

She wheeled around. "Is it?"

He wrapped an arm around her waist and pulled her back, the roar of desire she'd awakened in him still sounding so loud in his head, still pounding so hard in his veins, that he wondered whether it would be ever be quieted again. She let out a little yelp of surprise. Jake leaned down. "I don't want to kiss a princess," he said, his voice nearly a growl. "I want to kiss *you,* Mariabella. Only you."

Then he did exactly that again, this time taking no quarter with her, pouring the passion that had built up inside him for years into their embrace. Mariabella let out a mew, and grasped his shirt, curling her fists into his back. He hoisted her up onto the counter, his hands roaming her waist, her back, into her hair, unable to touch enough of her at once. He wanted more, he wanted all of her, right here, right now, but instead did the right thing and pulled back with a groan.

Her lips were swollen and red, her chest heaving with rapid breaths. "We…we probably should not…"

"Why not? Because you're a princess? I don't care about that." And as the words left his mouth, he realized he didn't. She was the same woman now, as she had been yesterday. Okay, so they'd have a few more bumps in their relationship to work around, but he could deal with that. He was alive again, for the first time in forever, and Jake refused to let that go, over something as small as royalty. "I told you, I loved Uccelli when I visited the country. Surely we could find a way to make this work."

"It is more than loving the country, Jake." She shook her head. "Someday, I will be *queen.* You would never be acceptable to my father as a king." She hung her head. "I am sorry, but duty must come first."

He let out a gust. "Duty? You sound like me now. I've spent five years putting duty and work ahead of living and now that I've met you, I've finally begun to realize what I'm missing out on. If you end this now, you will be missing out, too."

Outside, the storm had abated, and the wind stopped its assault on the little cottage. Mother Nature had quieted her war with the coast of Harborside, restoring it to its natural equilibrium.

She gripped the countertop. In her eyes, he saw resignation. "As a royal, my world is almost a…cage of expectations. You do not understand. I cannot have the life others can. I just cannot. Please make this easier on both of us, Jake, and—" she paused, tears filling her green eyes like rain puddling in a lake "—leave."

He stood his ground. He couldn't leave, not until he had the answer he'd come for, the one that had driven him out of the bar, and into her arms, the one answer he hadn't found in her artwork or in her kiss. "Why are you hiding here? And I don't mean just hiding from your name. I mean really hiding."

"What are you talking about? I am living my life."

"You talk about your life being a cage in Uccelli, and yet you've made a cage in Harborside, too."

"I live freely here."

"As yourself?"

"Of course not." She threw up her hands. "What, do you think this is all some fairy tale? That I can just be a princess and live happily ever after?"

"Why not?"

"It does not work that way. Not for me."

"Then how free are you, really, if you're afraid to fall in love? Afraid to be yourself?" He plucked a closed daisy out of the bouquet he had given her, and held it out. "You're like this flower. Shut off, tucked among the others. No one knows the power you hold, because you're just…hiding. You could change this town, make *real* changes, as Princess Mariabella, instead of just Mariabella Romano. You could bring it the kind of publicity it needs, the sort of business that would help these owners survive the other months of the year. And yet—"

She wrapped her arms around herself, anger spiking the color in her face. "And yet what?"

"You choose to be selfish and protect yourself instead of helping the people who have helped you."

"I am doing the least selfish thing possible. Putting this town ahead of everything that matters to me."

Jake laid the single flower on the table, beside one of Mariabella's sketches of a bird in flight. "Are you? Or are you doing the easiest thing possible?"

She advanced on him, her green eyes ablaze with frustration. "Who are you to say that to me? When all you have done since you have arrived in this town is take the easy road?

Followed the company line? Take your own risks, Jake Lattimore, and then tell me how to live my life."

He didn't respond. They'd said it all. Jake turned and left. The flower laid on the table, forgotten and wilting.

CHAPTER TEN

JAKE jerked awake, threw back the thick down comforter and got to his feet. Overnight, frost had coated the windows, blocking the view with a lacy spiderweb of white. Didn't matter. He didn't need to see Harborside to sketch out the plan in his head.

He crossed to the small desk in the corner of his room at the Seaside Inn, drew a pad of paper out of the briefcase sitting on the floor and began to write. At first, full sentences, then, as the frenzy to get it all down overtook him, short bullets, single words, just enough to jog his memory later.

A half hour later, Jake sat back and read over the pages he had composed. The board would undoubtedly think he was crazy. But this...

This would work.

He knew it. Deep in his gut, in that core knot that drove his best decisions, he knew, just knew, this was the decision that would make everyone happy. The company. The town. And most of all—

The princess.

A grin took over his face, the feeling of joy spreading through his chest, his veins. The emotion was so foreign, he nearly didn't recognize it. All these years, his heart had been as frozen as the icicles dangling from the peaks outside, and now—

The fiery woman from Uccelli had brought about a spring thaw. For the first time in forever, Jake imagined a different future. One with someone else in it.

One with Mariabella curled up in his arms, in front of the fireplace on Christmas Day. If he could make this idea work, maybe he could make that work, too.

She'd been right about him, damn it. And it felt real good to admit it.

His cell phone rang, and he flipped it out. "Dad! I was just about to call you. I've got an idea you have to hear."

"There was nothing on the fax machine this morning. No overnight delivery waiting for me. Nothing." His father's voice held a mixture of worry and disappointment. "We need this, Jake. Where are the real estate agreements for Harborside?"

"I'm working on it, Dad. Listen—"

His father sighed. "The board is pushing for me to hire an outsider."

While the mouse was away, the cats plotted. Jake shouldn't have been surprised. The board had always considered him, as the heir, nothing more than a nepotism appointment. "Don't worry about it. I have an idea for this town that can be great. Remember what you used to tell me about the old days, back when you started the company?"

"What do you mean?"

"The first resort you built. That one in New Jersey." Jake waited, allowing the memory a moment to travel across the phone line.

"You mean the inn? The one I took you to when you were—"

"Seven. And eight. And nine, because I begged you to."

His father chuckled, and something heavy that had been carried for so long in Lawrence Lattimore's heart seemed to flow out in that sound. "You loved that place."

"Everyone loved it."

"I have a lot of great memories of that place," his father said. "You and I, we used to take the rowboat out, remember? There was that great fishing hole, the one just you and I knew about. We had more than one dinner we caught ourselves from that place."

"I remember, Dad."

"And the hiking. Saw your first deer in those woods. You were six." His father chuckled. "I think you were more scared of it, than it was of you."

Jake laughed. "I remember that, too."

His father sighed. "It was too bad we couldn't have made that property more profitable. I hated selling it."

"Maybe if we'd handled the inn differently, Dad. Looked at the property from different angles. I think now, with some experience under our belts, we could turn a profit. I had some ideas this morning—"

"Jake, the time for inns like that has passed. Now everyone wants those fancy resorts. Cater to your every whim. Live like the rich do."

"Not everyone wants that, Dad. Some people want the simple life. To feel like..." Jake crossed to the window. He rubbed at the frosted pane with his palm, enough to open up a tiny view of the snowy street below. The garland hung between the street poles, the bows waving in the breeze, the neighbors heading to their shops, waving to one another. "To feel like they've gone home."

"When they go on vacation? Not anymore. I wish it wasn't so, but that's the reality of this business. The board says—"

Jake let out a gust. "Think outside the box, Dad. You used to do that, remember?" The Lawrence Lattimore who had founded the company had been a man who charged into deals, who thought with his gut, not with a team of accountants. But as the years wore on, and his father had had to report to more and more people, he'd become less like that, and more of a conformist in business.

"I wish I could. Those days, they were great, but…" His father's sigh seemed to weigh a hundred pounds. "They're over. It's time for me to put my feet up and watch from the sidelines."

Jake could hear the sadness in his father's voice. "What if you didn't have to? What if you could have the company you used to?"

"I don't live like that anymore. It's too crazy. Too risky."

Jake grinned. "Yeah, maybe it is. But I'm going to make it work right here. In Harborside."

"Son, you do that, and you'll ruin this company. We need something powerful. Something big, something that will take Lattimore back up to the top. Use the proven formula, Jake. Trust the board, not the ramblings of an old man who should be retired. We just can't take a risk. Not now."

"No, Dad. That's where you're wrong." Jake turned away from the window, and for the first time since he'd arrived in this town, felt as if everything was going to fall into place exactly right. "We need to go back to where we used to be, lead with our gut, not with the bean counters. That's our ticket to the top."

His father let out a sigh. "I don't know what's gotten into you. Tomorrow's Christmas Eve, Jake. Get this deal done, and fax me the deeds so we can break ground before February. That's the only present I want." His father hung up.

Jake would prove his father's theory wrong. One way or another. And in doing so, maybe he'd help Lawrence Lattimore find the business fire that had long ago died away.

The suitcase lay empty on Mariabella's bed.

Every item she put in, she took back out. She couldn't seem to pack anything. Not her jeans, not her sweaters, not her makeup, not her hairbrush. She clutched the plane ticket, sat on the edge of her bed and cried.

She couldn't do it. Simply couldn't do it. Just the thought of wearing that crown for the rest of her life made her want to run and hide. She looked out the window, at the view that had become as much a part of her as her own hand, and let out a sigh.

Then she made the call.

It took ten minutes before she was connected to the king, a flurry of activity, with people whispering on the other end, the rumors flying about the princess being in contact after her long, unexplained absence. "All I want to hear is when your flight is arriving so I can send Reynaldo to pick you up," her father said when he finally answered. No greeting. No "how are you."

Mariabella took in a breath, and steeled herself. "I'm not coming back, Papa."

She could have cut through the long, icy silence with a razor blade. "You will. I command it."

A year ago, a day ago, Mariabella would have backed down and agreed with her father. He was the king, after all, and she had learned from the day she was born never to disagree with the king.

Her gaze strayed to the Gerbera daisies, and her resolve steeled. She had to do the right thing. Not just for her, but for her country. Jake was right. She'd been hiding too long, from her true self. From what she really wanted. She'd played at being an ordinary woman, and never really done it.

How could she, if the entire time she'd lived in Harborside, she'd been living a lie? How could she ever know if she could be the kind of woman she wanted to be, unless she stepped up and did it as herself? As Mariabella Santaro?

"I can't," she said. "I won't make a good queen and you know it, Papa. My heart isn't in it. I don't think it ever was."

He snorted. "You think this position is about heart? It's *duty*, Mariabella. Now stop this silliness and return at once."

"You already have a daughter who wants to be queen, father. Let Allegra step up to the throne. And let me have my life. If you have ever loved me, even a little, then please, please, Papa—" her voice caught "—let me go."

Then she hung up the phone, and let the tears take over.

She was now a woman without a family or a country. But at least she was finally and truly free.

Jake had his argument ready before Mariabella even opened the door. "I know I'm the last person in the world you want to see right now, but I have a gift for you."

"A gift?"

He grinned. "It's Christmas. People give each other gifts."

She hesitated, and for a second, he thought she might close the door before he could talk to her. "Jake, Christmas isn't for two more days."

"So sue me for being early." He handed her a box, wrapped in bright red paper and topped with a white bow. "I just wanted to show you that I thought about what you said yesterday. And that you were right."

Despite everything, Mariabella smiled, and waved him into her house. One hurdle passed. Maybe there was hope for more. "Do you want some coffee?"

"I'd love some." Hell, he'd drink baby formula if it meant seeing her again.

She put down the box, then went into the kitchen and returned with two mugs of coffee and a small plate of raspberry thumbprint cookies. Then she sat down across from him to unwrap the gift. The bow slid easily off the top, fluttering to the floor. The box lid lifted off, then Mariabella tugged out the tissue-wrapped item inside and peeled away the white paper covering it. "This is…a dollhouse?"

"A mock-up. Of what I want to build here."

She glanced down again and saw, not a monster of a hotel,

like the one he had shown her in New York, but something closer to the inn they had visited in New Jersey. "It looks like…a house."

He grinned and nodded. "That's the plan. I want to put on a big front porch and a long, wide back porch. Lots of chairs, for looking out at the view of the ocean, then benches in the front so people can greet the locals when they walk by. Dinners will be served family style so that when you come and stay here, you'll be able to sit and get to know the other people who are staying in Harborside. There will be boating and swimming. No noisy Jet Skis. We'll have rooms designed with families in mind, and lots of family activities planned. It will be like the vacations from the old days, but taken up a few notches."

"You sound excited."

"I am." His smile widened. "It's all I've been able to think about for hours and hours. I had to drive to Boston this morning and pay a shop to create this—don't even ask me how much it cost—because I couldn't wait to show you my vision for Harborside."

She turned the mock-up around, then lifted it up and peeked inside the tiny windows, the itty-bitty door. She ran a finger down the roof line, along the slender poles of the porch. "This is perfect. I can just see it in town. It matches the buildings we already have, and even looks a little like the lighthouse, the way the posts curve on the porch here, and the colors that you used."

"I know."

She touched his hand, and fire exploded in her gut. "I did not think you noticed anything on the tour we took."

"It wasn't easy. I was a little distracted by my tour guide." His hand came up to cup her jaw, thumb teasing at her bottom lip. "More than a little distracted."

"All I did was show you some whales."

"You showed me far more than that, Mariabella." Her name slid off his tongue in a whisper, just before he closed the gap and kissed her. Then Jake drew back, and took her hand in his. "If you give me a chance, Mariabella, and support this, I promise, it will work out for the town, for you, for all the residents. This will be a resort that will fit Harborside. That world we saw in the room at the top of the stairs, that's the kind of world I want here. One where people come and they feel like they've come…"

"Home," she finished, the world escaping her on a breath. She glanced down again at the tiny building and saw in it the exact kind of vacation place she would have chosen. A retreat, a haven.

It was, as she'd said, home. Here in Harborside. She couldn't imagine it anywhere else.

"Exactly. When people look out the windows of their room, I want them to see the real Harborside. The one that *you* love." He tipped her chin until her gaze met his. "The one that you've taught me to love, too."

"You…love this town?"

"Lighthouse, boardwalk and all. It took me a while, but it grew on me." He grinned. "It helped that it had such a beautiful ambassador."

"Oh, I am not—"

"You are. Don't sell yourself short. From all accounts, from everyone I've talked to, you've done more for this town in the last year than anyone. Your enthusiasm has brought it back to life."

"But it has not been enough." She gestured out the window. "All your numbers said so, and so did you. I could have done more."

"But if you do, you'll give up part of your life," he said. "I had no right to say that yesterday. I didn't think about what the publicity would do to you. To the privacy that is so important to you." He laid a hand on top of the mock-up of the future resort. "This, however, can make the final difference for Harborside. It can fill in the financial gaps, without you having to be Princess Mariabella. You can be just Mariabella, as you've always been."

She rose and crossed to the fireplace. Beneath her, logs crackled and burned, releasing a cozy comfort. "Except…to make this resort work, you have to have real estate. In a good location, yes?"

"Yes."

They both knew what that meant. He was a businessman, one who wouldn't have reached the position of CEO if he hadn't employed winning strategies.

"The best location is on the boardwalk," Mariabella said, praying he'd disagree.

He didn't. "Yes."

She turned away from the fireplace and looked back at the miniature resort. In it, she saw thought. Caring. A man who had looked around the town she loved—and heard, not just her voice, but those of the other people who lived here.

"You can still have your gallery, I promise," Jake said, reaching for her, knowing what she was thinking. "There will be room for local businesses, every one of them who wants to stay, and even new ones who want to come to town. I'll build you the best and biggest gallery you've ever seen, right here. And give you a wonderful place to hang your art, when you're ready. I'm redesigning the entire complex to have a town-within-a-town feel. I want it to be a community, not just a hotel."

She met his gaze, and saw honesty, integrity, in his blue eyes. Jake Lattimore meant what he was saying. Excitement colored his words, and she knew that enthusiasm would spill over into the town, rejuvenating it in a way nothing else ever had. The boardwalk would be preserved, just in a different form. Everyone would win.

She had done all she could for Harborside, with the events,

the Community Development Committee, but there was much more this building could do. With the Lattimore Inn, Harborside could make that jump from nothing to something big. Everyone she cared about would be taken care of financially, while the town's setting would be preserved.

"Do you still have those papers?" she said.

"Mariabella—"

"Give them to me, Jake. I want to do this."

Without a word, he reached into the pocket of his suit jacket. Mariabella took the purchase and sales agreement from Jake, then she swallowed hard and decided for the first time in her life to take a chance and to trust someone other than herself.

She reached for a pen on the coffee table, then, before she could think twice, signed over ownership of her gallery.

Because she had fallen in love with Jake Lattimore. With the man who had found out she was a princess, and acted the same, who had listened to her when she'd talked about this town, and shown her that he could bring the dreams she had into a reality.

And most of all, because he had made her a promise she couldn't refuse. To take care of everything she loved—and make it even better than it already was.

CHAPTER ELEVEN

MARIABELLA rolled over on Christmas Eve morning, and stretched her full length on the double bed. She had plenty of time before she had to go to work, because the gallery was only open half the day, and Carmen had agreed to handle the morning shift, so that Mariabella could get the cooking done for dinner that night. As Mariabella lay in bed, she smiled.

Had she finally found a man to love?

One she could trust?

One who understood her?

Maybe there was a way to make all of this work after all. Maybe she could live an ordinary life. Live in peace and obscurity here in Harborside, with Jake. She could go on, as she was, without ever telling anyone her real identity.

Except…

Was Jake right? Was she hiding from herself?

But he didn't understand how the reporters could force her again into the very prison she had escaped. No, she would keep her identity secret for as long as possible.

Mariabella got to her feet. She drew her robe around her and started to head toward the shower.

That was when she heard the shouts.

Her name.

Rising in volume.

She halted. Pivoted toward the windows.

And saw what she'd dreaded all this time crowding onto the cottage's small driveway.

Dozens of reporters, their lenses trained on her house. Still cameras, video cameras, television trucks, live feeds—every type of media exposure and kind of media hound—were out there, just waiting to feed on her story.

She stumbled back and collapsed on the bed. No. How did they—

And then the realization slammed into her with the force of a hurricane.

The only one who knew her true identity was Jake.

The betrayal stung, hitting her as hard as a blow to the gut. She'd given up everything—and now she'd lost her trust, too.

Overnight, Harborside had quintupled in population. Jake stepped out of the Seaside Inn, and had to navigate past three television trucks and six rental cars before he could get close to the limo. He stopped in the middle of the street, dread sinking in his stomach. "Oh, God, Mariabella."

It took less than two minutes to track down the source of the leak about Mariabella's identity. Jake hadn't had to search any farther than the small café at the end of the boardwalk. He had to work hard to control the fury rising inside him. "How could you, Darcy?"

His marketing director stared at him like he had grown two heads. "You of all people should know, Jake. This is business, pure and simple. I can't believe *you* didn't do this. My God, you have a perfect opportunity to exploit here and bring a huge amount of publicity to the project. Think about it. A real, honest-to-God princess? Associated with our hotel? You couldn't *pay* for that kind of exposure. The company needs that. When I called New York—"

"Called who in New York? Exactly?"

Crimson filled her cheeks. She dropped her hand to the table and toyed with her silverware.

"What am I missing here?"

"I...I can't tell you."

"What do you mean, you can't tell me?"

Darcy bit her lip, then finally lifted her head. "I don't work for you. I never really did."

And then he knew. The board. Carl Winters showing up, checking on his progress. His father, worried and stressed, mentioning how the board had been pressuring him to hire an outsider. A group of ten men, thinking they could rule the world, simply because they were the board of directors of the corporation.

No longer. Jake would make sure of that.

"And now you don't work for me at all. Darcy, you're fired." Jake exploded out of the seat and stalked out of the restaurant. He wanted to hit a wall, to punch out the nearest window, but more, he wanted to drive up to New York and confront every person in the company. Now.

The minute he hit the street, the reporters leapt on him like dogs on a bone.

"Mr. Lattimore! Did you know you were dating a princess?"

"Mr. Lattimore, how does it feel to have a princess as the spokesperson for the newest Lattimore Resort?"

"Mr. Lattimore, are you going to invite the royal family to the opening of the new hotel?"

The microphones came at him, fast, furious weapons. He put up his arms, fending them off, and ignored the questions, barreling forward through the crush of reporters. They kept up their assault.

"Mr. Lattimore, is it true the new architectural design is based on Uccelli Castle?" A reporter stepped in front of him and waved a newspaper in his face. "Do you have a comment on this article about the design?"

Jake grabbed the paper out of the man's hand. "No. Get out of my way."

"Are you exploiting Princess Mariabella?" another reporter shouted.

He shoved past all of them, and opened the door of the gallery. The reporters moved to follow him inside, but Jake turned around and gave them a look that said not to even try it. They must have read the menace in his face, because they backed off, hanging outside the door like a pack of hungry dogs.

Jake vowed to make every member of the board pay for what they had done to Mariabella. If it was this bad here, outside the gallery, he could only imagine the circus outside her house. He'd do what he could to control the damage. If it wasn't too late.

"Boy, are your stars out of alignment." Carmen, Mariabella's assistant, strode forward, one fist on her slim hip, and shook her head.

"Excuse me?"

"You've made a mess of this. It was all going well, and then wham, you made it as wrong as wrong can be."

"I didn't—" He let out a breath. Explaining the internal subterfuge in Lattimore Properties to Carmen wouldn't solve the big problem. He needed to talk to Mariabella. "Is Mariabella here?"

"She won't talk to you. I don't blame her. You're like a meteor crashing into her planet."

"I have to talk to her, Carmen. I…I didn't do this." He waved at the throng of media outside. "She has to understand that."

Carmen considered him for a long, long moment. Then she let out a sigh, and nodded. "She's not coming in today, and I can't say I blame her. But come to dinner at her house. Tonight. A lot of her friends from town will be there. I have to go to my mother's, but don't worry," Carmen said, grinning, "you'll have a fan club for back up."

Mariabella's house, with the rest of the Harborside residents? All of whom probably blamed him for this mess. Sounded more like a lynch mob to Jake. "I don't know—"

"I do know," Carmen said. "I know this town, and I know Mariabella. And I know what Mariabella's horoscope said for today." She leaned forward, as if she were about to whisper a secret to Jake. "It said she should prepare for a surprise visitor at a gathering. You—" she gave Jake a little swat on the shoulder "—are the surprise visitor. And her Christmas Eve dinner is the gathering. See? It's all in the stars."

He didn't know about stars, or anything being foretold by some newspaper column, but reasoned talking to Mariabella with the crush of reporters outside—and the possibility of them crashing the conversation at any time—made little sense. Better to wait until later. With any luck, even the media would go home for Christmas Eve, and he could find some time alone with Mariabella.

And find an explanation for what had happened.

Cletus sat at the head of the table, Zeke at the opposite end. Louisa sat on one side, while Louisa's dog, George, ran between the legs of the kitchen chairs, hoping for a stray crumb or two. The media onslaught had ebbed slightly, but a good half-dozen dogged reporters still sat outside, determined to talk to Mariabella. She'd finally called the Harborside police chief, and asked him to remind them about the rules of trespassing. That had at least pushed the reporters back, but not sent them away.

As for Jake—

She tried not to think about him. If she did, she wouldn't make it through the day. It was Christmas Eve, and she was going to enjoy her holiday with her friends, even as her heart broke a little more with each passing hour.

"You sure know how to treat us right," Cletus said. "You

make me think I might want to settle down with a woman someday."

Louisa snorted. "You'd have to find a woman who'd take you first."

Cletus shot her a grin. "I'm an eligible bachelor, with a unique home. Any woman in her right mind would love to have me."

Louisa shook her head and tossed her dog a piece of bread crust.

Across from them, Zeke shifted in his chair, and fiddled with his napkin. "If no one else is going to talk about the elephant in the room, I'll do it."

"My dog is not fat!" Louisa smacked Zeke's arm. "He's…husky."

Zeke rolled his eyes. "I meant the princess, Louisa, not George."

"Oh. Well, then, fine. It's just that George is sensitive about his weight." Louisa soothed the dachshund with a pat on the back and a tidbit of bread.

Zeke shook his head, then directed his attention toward Mariabella. "I think I speak for everyone when I say I don't care whether you're a princess, or the last Romanov, or the forgotten stepchild of the Kennedys. To us, you're just Mariabella. So, there."

Mariabella glanced around the table, taking in the faces of these people who had become her friends, her extended family, who had welcomed her into their hearts, their homes, their lives, and now were accepting her as she was, without reservations. "I…I do not know what to say."

"Well then, say grace, for Pete's sake," Cletus said. "We want to eat."

Mariabella laughed, then dropped her head and whispered a prayer, that included gratitude for her friends and for this town. Everyone around the table issued an Amen, and then they began to pass the platters of food, chatting as they dished up generous helpings of lasagna and roasted root vegetables. Conversations flowed as naturally today as they had on any other day.

Except for Cletus. He seemed to hang back, a little more reserved than usual. Mariabella handed him a basket of rolls. "Cletus, is something bothering you?"

He squirmed in his seat. "I don't want to talk about it. Not today."

"If it is about me being the princess of Uccelli—"

"It's not." He scowled. Looked at Zeke, who shook his head, as if warning him not to say what he was going to say. Cletus squirmed some more. "Aw, damn. I was going to let it go, but I can't. You have to know, Mariabella."

Cletus reached into his back pocket and pulled out a page from a Boston newspaper. The article was small, probably inserted at the last minute, among all the holiday stories. But the headline—

The headline stopped Mariabella's heart. Froze her blood.

Lattimore Properties to Build Megahotel in Harborside.

No. He'd promised. He wouldn't—

Would he?

But the words were there, in black and white. Showing Jake Lattimore to be a liar.

And Mariabella to be a fool. A fool taken in by a charming smile and a story a mile long. He'd done far worse than just call the media and tell them who she was. He'd betrayed her, on every single level.

She scanned the article, until the words began to swim in her vision. "Fifteen stories…richly appointed…similar to properties in New York and Miami…offering Jet Ski rental… tiki huts and poolside bar service."

Oh, God, how could he? She had believed him, trusted him.

But worse, she had fallen in love with him. How could she have been so stupid?

She knew better, oh, how she knew better.

Mariabella dropped the article to the table, then glanced up at Cletus, and at Zeke. Wishing they would tell her the whole thing was a joke, some kind of ruse planted by the media to get her riled up.

But the two men nodded slowly. "I checked out the article on the newswires," Zeke said, "before I came over today. It's all over the place. They made the announcement late last night. I read the press release, right on the corporate Web site, Mariabella."

Her mouth worked, trying to form the words. "Did…did the press release have a time on it?"

"It was posted just after eleven o'clock."

An hour after Jake had left last night. After he had shown her that mock-up of a home-like setting for the resort he would build in Harborside. After he had made all these promises—and she had believed them.

And after she had signed over her gallery to him.

She'd thought the hurt couldn't get worse. Thought the pain she'd felt this morning, when she'd seen the media camped outside her house, couldn't run any deeper.

She'd been wrong.

"He promised me he would not do this," she whispered.

"I'm sorry," Zeke said quietly. "I thought he was a good man. I really did."

A tear dropped onto the newspaper, blurring the print into a puddle of black letters. "Me, too."

Louisa's dog scrambled to his feet, nails clacking on the wood floors, and started yapping. He ran for the door, tail wagging, a little brown alarm bell ringing before the doorbell did.

A gust of frustration escaped Mariabella at the sound of the chimes. Just what she didn't need right now—an intrusion from the media. "I am going to call the police chief again. And have him throw those people in prison." Throw Jake in there while he was at it, for good measure.

"I'll help you," Cletus grumbled. "Damned idiots keep interrupting my dinner."

Mariabella opened the door, a tirade prepared for the rude reporter on her doorstep. But she found instead the last two people she'd expected to see in Harborside.

Her parents.

"Mama. Papa. What are you doing here?"

Behind Mariabella, Cletus, Zeke and Louisa gasped. Louisa whispered something about the king and queen.

En masse, the reporters swarmed toward the house, questions spewing from their mouths, as rapid fire as machine guns. Mariabella waved her parents inside, then shut and locked the door. The shouting continued for several minutes, then finally died down as the media realized they weren't going to get an answer. Mariabella double-checked the curtains, ensuring there wasn't an opening for a stray photograph. "I'm sorry. They found out who I am."

Her father's lips pursed. It gave Franco Santaro, normally a tall, distinguished man with white hair and a trim frame, a pinched, bitter look. "I know. All the more reason to come home. Now." He spoke in their native language, keeping the conversation between the three of them.

"I'm sorry you came all the way to America to drag me back, instead of to see me for Christmas," Mariabella said. Of course her father wouldn't fly across the world for a holiday visit, but to demand her return. To tell her he didn't accept her refusal of the crown. Disappointment sunk like a stone in her gut. "It doesn't matter, Papa. I'm not leaving."

"Cara," her mother said, reaching for her daughter, and shooting her husband a sharp look, "we miss you."

"I miss you too, Mama," Mariabella said, the sentiment tearing her throat as she drew her mother's generous frame into a short hug, "but I can't go home and be queen. I'll never be happy. Here, I'm happy."

Her father waved a hand in dismissal. "Childish notions. Come to your senses, Mariabella. There is a car waiting. We'll send for your things."

Had he heard nothing she'd said in that phone call? Why was she even surprised? Her father hadn't heard a word she'd said in twenty-five years. Why would he start now? "Why won't you listen to me, Papa? I won't go. I have found a life here. A life that means something."

"Your life as queen will mean more."

She sighed. "Yes, maybe it would. But what kind of queen would I be, if my heart forever lay elsewhere?"

Her father shook his head and muttered under his breath.

"Papa." Mariabella reached for her father's arm, trying for once to reach him as her father, not as the king. Not caring about decorum, about him being the monarch. They were on American soil now, and if she had learned one thing in all the months she had spent here, it was that relationships were built on connections—physical and emotional—and when she held herself back from those connections, she lost out on everything that mattered.

Except, with Jake Lattimore, she had connected, and lost anyway. Maybe she should have taken a page from her father's book and maintained her emotional distance.

But no. That coldness had hurt her too much over the years. Better to love and hurt than to go on living with this empty hole, waiting for love to fill it.

"Papa," she said again.

His gaze met hers, but he didn't say anything.

"Haven't you ever wanted anything other than to be king?"

Surprise lit his light green eyes. "I've…I've never thought about it."

Bianca gave her husband a knowing stare. "Franco."

"That was a long time ago," he said to his wife.

"Tell your daughter the truth."

He shifted his weight, looking so much like an ordinary man in that moment, that Mariabella wanted to reach out and hug him. But one did not do that to the king of Uccelli, so she refrained. Time ticked by, her father delaying and looking like he'd rather be sitting through a ten-hour speech than answering the question. Finally, he cleared his throat and spoke. "Once—for a moment only—I thought I could be a musician."

He could have hit her with a trombone and she would have been less surprised. "A musician? You don't even play an instrument."

"I did. When I was younger. And I had time. Now my days are filled with the monarchy. With more important duties."

Mariabella looked at her mother, who nodded and smiled, then back at her father. "What…what did you play?"

He shifted his weight again. "The drums. I fancied myself in a band some day."

"You. In a band?"

He waved off the thought. "It was a crazy idea I had for maybe five minutes, then I remembered my duty to the crown. Or, rather, my father reminded me of my duty." He gave her a pointed look. "As should you."

Her mother's gaze connected with hers, soft wisdom in her deep green eyes, shaded by long hair the same color as her daughter's. "Show him, *cara*. Show him what you dream."

"Bianca, talk sense into our daughter. Don't encourage her to—"

"Franco, you promised to listen and not to talk so much." Bianca put a hand on her hip. "You are too much a king and too little a father. See her as your daughter for once, and not as the future queen." She gave her husband a little push, and he stumbled a few steps forward into Mariabella's living room.

Mariabella's guests let out a surprised "ooh."

Annoyance filled the king's features. "Bianca, do you forget who I am?"

"No, I do not," she said. "You are Mariabella's father and my husband before you are anything else. Now take off your crown and act like it."

From across the room, a second collective gasp escaped the group. They might not have understood the language, but they definitely caught the translation of the tension. When Mariabella glanced over, all three heads of her guests swiveled away, and they got busy eating.

Bianca nodded toward her husband. "Do it, Franco. Or you will be flying home alone."

"Bianca, this is insanity." He pursed his lips again, then relented. "All right."

Her mother walked away, and crossed to the kitchen table, slipping into the seat vacated by Mariabella. She said hello to Cletus, Zeke and Louisa, then buttered a roll, and started talking to them about their plans for Christmas, as if they had been her neighbors forever. Once the other three got over their initial shock, the conversation flowed as easily as a river.

Mariabella waved her father over to the sofa, the two of them taking seats on opposite ends. The fire crackled happily, the scent of the wood accented by a cinnamon apple candle burning on the end table. "I'm not changing my mind, Papa. I can't be queen. I'm sorry."

Even though it would be easy to run back to Uccelli. To hide from the media onslaught. To flee from what had happened with Jake. To bury herself in the monarchy, and let that take over her broken heart. After all, she had nothing tying her to this town anymore. She'd sold her gallery, given up her livelihood. If she stayed in Harborside, she'd only watch it become a nightmarish version of the town she loved.

Going back to Uccelli, though, would force her back into the same cage she had fled. No matter what heartbreak this town held, it still offered something she would never find wearing the crown.

Freedom.

Her father draped his hands over his knees and let out a sigh. "I am disappointed, but I understand," he said quietly. "My illness made me think about all the years I have spent as the monarch. They were hard years. But years I wouldn't trade, you know that, don't you?"

"You have been a good king, Papa. Everything I learned from you, I used to help this town grow and prosper. Leadership, diplomacy, organization. It's worked here, and been…fun." She smiled. "I just don't want to do the same thing from the confines of a kingdom."

The wood popped and sizzled in the fire. The elf and Santa clock on the mantel ticked the time away. In the background, the stereo played soft, instrumental versions of Christmas songs. "You have to love the job and the monarchy, to do it right." The king gazed at his daughter for a long time. "You do know what you are giving up?"

She nodded.

He raised his gaze to the ceiling, as if looking for answers from the heavens. Then he paused, and rose. "This is yours?"

Her father's attention had lighted on the painting of the two pelicans. After Jake had left the other day, Mariabella had framed and hung the piece. For too long, she had, as Jake had said, held back from displaying her art—her soul. She had left the rest of the pieces at the framer's, intending to have them readied for a show in January. Except now she no longer owned the gallery, and the building would undoubtedly be demolished by then.

No matter. She'd exhibit either way. Mariabella Santaro was tired of hiding. From her name, from her art. "Yes, it is."

"I had no idea." Her father moved closer, reaching up a hand to trace the outline of the three-dimensional birds. "You have a good eye. An even better hand."

In all the years she had been painting, and going to college pursuing her art degree, her father had expressed nothing but disdain for her passion. He'd seen it as a waste of her time, a distraction from her destiny on the throne. Maybe today, with the revelation of his own dreams, he'd begun to understand her better. "Thank you, Papa."

"This…this is what you want to do?"

"That, and continue my work helping this town. I've made a difference here. A small one, but still, a difference." Yet, if Harborside changed as it would under the Lattimore property, would she stay here? Or move to a place like Harborside used to be?

Her father turned and smiled at her. A genuine smile, one that came from his heart. "I have heard about your work. Your committees, your dances and events. All from your mother, who keeps me apprised."

"Mama tells you what I do?"

He nodded. "I am proud, Mariabella. I don't think I have told you." Her father considered her for a long time, his gaze at first harsh and judgmental, all king. Then his eyes softened, and she saw another man take over, one she had glimpsed so rarely over the years she'd wondered if he really existed. A smile inched across his face, as if carving new territory. "So, you have a little of me in you after all?"

She returned his smile, and reached out a hand toward her father. He took hers, and their touch formed a bridge, a tentative one. "Yes, I think I do."

She saw what she thought might be tears in his eyes, but maybe was just a trick of the dancing firelight. "Then stay," he said. "Have the life I never did."

"You can still have that life, Papa."

"Ah, I am an old man, and the kingdom requires a king to be a certain kind of person."

"Says who? If there is one thing I've learned here, it's that life is in the living of your days, not in the dreaming about living them. A king can play the drums if he wants to," Mariabella said. "After all, he's the king. He makes all the rules."

Her father laughed, and in that sound, Mariabella heard the beginnings of a new relationship between the two of them. She caught her mother's eye. Bianca smiled, and gave her daughter a small nod. They weren't kings or queens or princesses at that moment, merely a family that was beginning to work out its kinks.

CHAPTER TWELVE

"GIVE me your tie."

Will put the limo in Park, and turned around in the driver's seat. "My tie?"

"I would have bought my own, but I've been a little busy. I'll give it back, I promise. Better yet, I'll buy you two dozen for Christmas."

Will shook his head, laughing, then undid his tie and tossed it over the seat. "You really want to wear dancing Santas?"

Jake glanced at Mariabella's cottage. The earlier snowstorm had kissed the entire house with a coating of white. Her Christmas lights twinkled like tiny sprites in the drifts piled on the shrubbery. Smoke curled from the chimney, scenting the air with the perfume of home. Of everything he'd ever wanted. "Yeah. I do."

"Good luck," Will said. "I'll pull the car over there to wait."

Jake shook his head. "No. Go home, Will. I'll see you on January fourth."

Will gaped at his boss. "January fourth? That's…that's almost two weeks off."

"With pay. Go to Jamaica or something with your wife, stay in the best Lattimore property we have. Don't call me, don't send a postcard, just enjoy yourself."

"What about you?"

Jake opened the limo door and stepped into the cold. "I've got a Christmas miracle to pull off."

He drew his coat tighter, then took a deep breath and strode up the walkway to Mariabella's door. He rang the bell, she opened the door—and nearly slammed it again in his face. "I do not have anything to say to you."

Jake put a hand on the oak frame. "I just want to talk to you for five minutes, Mariabella."

"Why? So you can tell me why you betrayed me? I saw the article." She started to shut the door, but he stopped it with his foot. "Just leave, Jake."

"Not until you hear me out." His gaze met hers. The fire in her green eyes sparked, then ebbed.

A bit.

Maybe there was still hope. God, he prayed there was.

Mariabella let out a gust. "Fine. Five minutes." She opened the door and let him in. Cletus, Zeke and Louisa sat at the kitchen table like a posse, shooting him death glares. Even George the dachshund let out a little growl from under the table. Two other people Jake didn't recognize sat on the sofa by the fireplace, sipping coffee.

She saw him glance at the strangers, and with clear reluctance, introduced him. "Jake Lattimore, these are my parents, Bianca and Franco Santaro."

The king and queen of Uccelli? Here in Harborside?

The king had the regal appearance of a man who had ruled for a long time. He sat stiffly, his white hair and defined features making him look imposing, strong. The queen, on the other hand, had more of Mariabella's features, and a softness to her green eyes that seemed to welcome Jake.

Jake crossed to them, and put out his hand, then gave a slight bow. "It's an honor to meet you, Your Majesties."

The queen looked from her daughter then to Jake. "Ah, this is the one for you, is it not, Mariabella?"

The king shot Jake a protective father glare.

"No." Mariabella scowled. "He is no one." She tugged Jake away from the living room and into a small bedroom off to the right. Dead silence fell over the living room. Mariabella shut the door, blocking any attempts at eavesdropping.

Mariabella flicked on the light switch, and illuminated a wide picture window that faced the ocean, then an easel in the center of the room, and a stack of empty canvases along the wall. A half-finished painting of an eagle sat on the easel. Her studio. "You have four and a half minutes," she said.

Okay. So she had no intentions of going easy on him. What had he expected, really?

"Put out your hands."

"What?"

"Just put out your hands."

She did as he asked, cupping her hands together. Jake reached into his coat pocket, then released a pile of something white. As the flecks fluttered down, Mariabella first thought he had dropped snowflakes into her hand, then realized the white pieces were shredded bits of paper. "What…what's this?"

"Every one of the purchase and sales agreements signed by the business owners of Harborside. Including you."

She stared at the pile in her hands. Then him. "Why would you do this? I thought you needed these lots to build your hotel."

"I did, until the board double-crossed me. They pressured my father into going in another direction, and used both of us to get what they wanted. You saw the newspaper article, right?"

She nodded.

"I had nothing to do with that. Nor did I tell the media who you were. That was all Darcy, and the board at Lattimore Properties, trying to exploit every angle they could for 'the good of the company.'" The air quotes and sarcasm in his voice made his feelings clear.

She glanced out the window behind her, the one that faced

the side yard. No curtains hung there, and she half expected a flash bulb to go off, broadcasting a private moment to the world.

"They're gone, Mariabella. And those reporters won't get within a hundred yards of you. Ever. I hired a security detail to keep them away. You can go on living your life here."

The media had left. Her life could return to the way it had been. Private, quiet. She owned her gallery again. She should have been happy.

But she wasn't.

An emptiness invaded her, something still missing, a piece of herself she had yet to find.

She dumped the pile of papers onto the small desk in the corner of her studio. "Why would you do that? You will get fired, Jake."

"No, I won't. My father and I together are the ones in charge now. We just had to join forces and eliminate the board. As a team, we own fifty-one percent of the company. It took a little doing to remind my father of who he used to be, and how we could go back to the kind of company we were. But now he's excited, charged up in a way I haven't seen him in years. He hadn't lost his touch, simply his passion for his job." Jake took Mariabella by the shoulders and drew her over to the large picture window. He pointed to the red light skimming across the water, the telltale sign of a boat riding through the channel. "Zeke issued a challenge to me the first day I was here. He told me I could be like a motorboat, churning up everything in my path, or like a sailboat, leaving the world relatively unchanged after I was here."

"And which have you chosen?" She held her breath, sure she knew the answer, but needing to ask the question anyway.

He leaned down, placing his face beside hers, cheeks meeting. "The sailboat, building an inn that fits Harborside, fits the people, fits the vision of those who love this place. We'll show every business owner, and be sure they all want to be on board, before they sign new agreements. Start at square one, and get community input. Make it a true Harborside property."

She turned in his arms, her gaze meeting his blue eyes. "What if it fails, like the last one?"

He shrugged. "We'll cross that bridge when we get to it. But I have a good feeling about this."

Mariabella's gaze drifted to the eagle half-finished on the painting sitting on her easel. Even birds had a nest to come back to, a place where they roosted, a home they built and tended lovingly. It wasn't just about how far they could soar, but about whether they could fly back to where they wanted to be.

And where she wanted to be was right here. As herself, not as Mariabella Romano. Not as a woman lying every day of her life. There was, as Jake had said, no freedom in lies. "Would it help if a princess ran an art gallery at the inn?"

"Mariabella, you don't have to do that. You can go on being Mariabella Romano. Keep your life the way it is."

"It is no life at all," she said. "Not if I am being someone else. I do not have to be queen to make a difference. I can do it as a princess."

He traced the outline of her jaw, and smiled. "And as a wife."

Had she heard him right? "A wife?"

"I've fallen in love with you, Mariabella. With you, not you the princess, or you, the gallery owner, but just *you*. And I don't want to do any of this—" he swept a hand toward the beach, the town "—without you. You are the dream I was looking for outside my window. And now that I've found you, I don't want to let you go."

A tear escaped and slid down her cheek. "I…I do not know what to say." He'd told her everything she'd always wanted to hear, and the words hummed in her heart.

Jake dropped to one knee, pulled a velvet box out of his pocket and held it open. A simple round diamond glittered back at her. Nothing ostentatious, nothing overdone. The perfect ring. "Say you'll marry me."

Had she once thought there were no Prince Charmings left in the world? That fairy tales didn't come true? She had been wrong, and she'd never been so glad to be wrong in her life. "Yes, Jake, yes, I'll marry you."

He rose, and swung her into his arms. They kissed, at the same time a light snow began to fall outside. The clock struck midnight, and Christmas began. But neither of them noticed, because they both already had the present they'd dreamed of—a present, and a future, with each other.

EPILOGUE

THE palace's landscaper had spent a month finding the perfect tree. He'd hemmed and hawed, until the queen herself had gone out to the woods and chosen the one that now stood proudly in the center hall. Dozens of people had come to see the big event.

"Ah, it is beautiful, isn't it?" Mariabella said to her sister. She stepped back and took in the entire twenty-five-foot-high pine, amazed at the perfect symmetry of the branches, the deep emerald color, offset by the white and gold decorations. Surrounded by the black-and-white marble floors, the two-story hand-carved wood walls, featuring reliefs of Uccelli's history, and the massive windows draped with thick red velvet curtains, the tree stood as an elaborate centerpiece to the castle's main gallery.

Allegra smiled. "It is. But it's still missing something." She handed the final ornament to her eldest sister.

"Shouldn't the queen do this job? After all, I live in America now."

Allegra shook her head, causing her crown to move slightly. The multicolored jewels ringing the gold headpiece sparkled under the pendant lights hanging from the massive, two-story ceiling. "As long as you are home, Mariabella, it is your job."

Mariabella drew her sister into a hug. "You will make a

wonderful queen." Allegra's coronation had been only last week, and the ceremony had been wonderful. Mariabella knew the moment she saw her sister accept the crown, that she had made the right decision in abdicating. Allegra had the passion for the job, the love of the monarchy, and the fortitude for the hard years ahead.

Allegra wiped a tear off her face. "Well, as queen, I am ordering you to hurry up. We have a wedding to go to."

Mariabella laughed, then crossed to the tree and hung the delicate crystal filigree angel on the tree. She stepped over to the wall, then flicked the switch. Thousands of tiny white lights sprang to life, bathing the center room of the castle in a golden light. A collective "ahh" went up among the crowd gathered around the tree.

"It is time, Mariabella." The king touched his daughter on the shoulder.

She nodded, then turned toward her father. He looked younger since he had stepped down and handed over the throne to his middle daughter, happier even. He laid a hand on top of his daughter's arm. "You look like your mother did forty years ago. Beautiful."

"Thank you, Papa."

"You will visit? Often?"

She nodded, tears choking her throat. "Of course. Jake not only loves my family, he loves the Uccelli wine. And you can only buy that here."

Her father laughed. "Then we shall keep on bottling it. By the gallon, if it brings you home more often. I miss you, Mariabella."

"I miss you too, Papa." She had returned to Uccelli a half-dozen times in the past year, and her parents had visited Harborside twice, staying at the Harborside Inn both times, and generating a little media storm with each visit. They'd loved the homey setting, even though it was a major departure from castle life, and vowed to return often. Mariabella had a feeling she and Jake would be putting a lot of miles on his private jet in the years to come.

The bridal march began to play, the organ music swelling and filling the main gallery. Mariabella and her father began the long walk down the hall, along a path littered with white daisies and crimson rose petals.

Candles lit the hall, which had been draped in pine garland and massive crimson bows. White silk shantung hung from ceiling to floor, making it feel as if they'd walked into a winter wonderland.

Jake stood in the chapel, waiting for her, flanked by Will, then Zeke and Cletus. On the bride's side, Allegra had taken her place as maid of honor, followed by Carlita and Carmen. A thousand more white candles flickered in the chapel, the only light for the small room. Beautiful, intimate and as close to a winter setting as she could get. The train of her dress swished along the path, with her veil fluttering softly at her back.

Her father placed a soft kiss on her cheek, then led her to Jake. The wedding march came to an end, and the guests began to take their seats. Neither Jake nor Mariabella noticed anything but each other.

Mariabella took her husband-to-be's hand and smiled, first at the snowman tie he wore, then at him. He matched her smile with one of his own. "I am the luckiest man in the world," he whispered.

"Because you are marrying the princess?"

"No." He placed a soft kiss against her lips. "Because in every fairy tale, the ending is always, 'And they lived happily ever after.' And that, my love, is exactly what I intend to do with you."

* * * * *

*Celebrate 60 years of pure reading pleasure with
Harlequin®!*

To commemorate the event, Silhouette Special Edition
invites you to Ashley O'Ballivan's bed-and-breakfast in
the small town of Stone Creek. The beautiful innkeeper
will have her hands full caring for her old flame Jack
McCall. He's on the run and recovering from a mysterious illness, but that won't stop him from trying to win
Ashley back.

*Enjoy an exclusive glimpse of Linda Lael Miller's
AT HOME IN STONE CREEK
Available in November 2009
from Silhouette Special Edition®*

The helicopter swung abruptly sideways in a dizzying arch, setting Jack McCall's fever-ravaged brain spinning.

His friend's voice sounded tinny, coming through the earphones. "You belong in a hospital," he said. "Not some backwater bed-and-breakfast."

All Jack really knew about the virus raging through his system was that it wasn't contagious, and there was no known treatment for it besides a lot of rest and quiet. "I don't like hospitals," he responded, hoping he sounded like his normal self. "They're full of sick people."

Vince Griffin chuckled but it was a dry sound, rough at the edges. "What's in Stone Creek, Arizona?" he asked. "Besides a whole lot of nothin'?"

Ashley O'Ballivan was in Stone Creek, and she was a whole lot of somethin', but Jack had neither the strength nor the inclination to explain. After the way he'd ducked out six months before, he didn't expect a welcome, knew he didn't deserve one. But Ashley, being Ashley, would take him in whatever her misgivings.

He had to get to Ashley; he'd be all right.

He closed his eyes, letting the fever swallow him.

There was no telling how much time had passed when he became aware of the chopper blades slowing overhead.

Dimly, he saw the private ambulance waiting on the airfield outside of Stone Creek; it seemed that twilight had descended.

Jack sighed with relief. His clothes felt clammy against his flesh. His teeth began to chatter as two figures unloaded a gurney from the back of the ambulance and waited for the blades to stop.

"Great," Vince remarked, unsnapping his seat belt. "Those two look like volunteers, not real EMTs."

The chopper bounced sickeningly on its runners, and Vince, with a shake of his head, pushed open his door and jumped to the ground, head down.

Jack waited, wondering if he'd be able to stand on his own. After fumbling unsuccessfully with the buckle on his seat belt, he decided not.

When it was safe the EMTs approached, following Vince, who opened Jack's door.

His old friend Tanner Quinn stepped around Vince, his grin not quite reaching his eyes.

"You look like hell warmed over," he told Jack cheerfully.

"Since when are you an EMT?" Jack retorted.

Tanner reached in, wedged a shoulder under Jack's right arm and hauled him out of the chopper. His knees immediately buckled, and Vince stepped up, supporting him on the other side.

"In a place like Stone Creek," Tanner replied, "everybody helps out."

They reached the wheeled gurney, and Jack found himself on his back.

Tanner and the second man strapped him down, a process that brought back a few bad memories.

"Is there even a hospital in this place?" Vince asked irritably from somewhere in the night.

"There's a pretty good clinic over in Indian Rock," Tanner answered easily, "and it isn't far to Flagstaff." He paused to help his buddy hoist Jack and the gurney into the back of the ambulance. "You're in good hands, Jack. My wife is the best veterinarian in the state."

Jack laughed raggedly at that.

Vince muttered a curse.

Tanner climbed into the back beside him, perched on some kind of fold-down seat. The other man shut the doors.

"You in any pain?" Tanner said as his partner climbed into the driver's seat and started the engine.

"No." Jack looked up at his oldest and closest friend and wished he'd listened to Vince. Ever since he'd come down with the virus—a week after snatching a five-year-old girl back from her non-custodial parent, a small-time Colombian drug dealer—he hadn't been able to think about anyone or anything but Ashley. When he *could* think, anyway.

Now, in one of the first clearheaded moments he'd experienced since checking himself out of Bethesda the day before, he realized he might be making a major mistake. Not by facing Ashley—he owed her that much and a lot more. No, he could be putting her in danger, putting Tanner and his daughter and his pregnant wife in danger, too.

"I shouldn't have come here," he said, keeping his voice low.

Tanner shook his head, his jaw clamped down hard as though he was irritated by Jack's statement.

"This is where you belong," Tanner insisted. "If you'd had sense enough to know that six months ago, old buddy, when you bailed on Ashley without so much as a fare-thee-well, you wouldn't be in this mess."

Ashley. The name had run through his mind a million times in those six months, but hearing somebody say it out loud was like having a fist close around his insides and squeeze hard.

Jack couldn't speak.

Tanner didn't press for further conversation.

The ambulance bumped over country roads, finally hitting smooth blacktop.

"Here we are," Tanner said. "Ashley's place."

* * * * *

Will Jack be able to patch things up with Ashley,
or will his past put the woman he loves in harm's way?
Find out in
AT HOME IN STONE CREEK
by Linda Lael Miller
Available November 2009
from Silhouette Special Edition®

This November,
Silhouette Special Edition®
brings you

NEW YORK TIMES
BESTSELLING AUTHOR

LINDA LAEL MILLER

At Home in Stone Creek

*Available in November
wherever books are sold.*

Visit Silhouette Books at www.eHarlequin.com

SSELLM60BPA

HARLEQUIN *Romance*

This November,
queen of the rugged rancher

PATRICIA THAYER

teams up with

DONNA ALWARD

to bring you an extra-special treat
this holiday season—

two romantic stories in one book!

Join sisters Amelia and Kelley for Christmas at
Rocking H Ranch where these feisty cowgirls swap
presents for proposals, mistletoe for marriage and
experience the unbeatable rush of falling in love!

Available in November wherever books are sold.

www.eHarlequin.com

HR17619

nocturne™

TIME RAIDERS

THE PROTECTOR

by *USA TODAY* bestselling author

MERLINE LOVELACE

Former USAF officer Cassandra Jones's unique psychic
skills come in handy, as she has been selected to join the
elite Time Raiders squad. Her first mission is to travel
back to seventh-century China to locate the final piece
of a missing bronze medallion. Major Max Brody is
assigned to accompany her, and soon Cassandra and
Max have to fight their growing attraction to each
other while the mission suddenly turns deadly....

Available November
wherever books are sold.

www.silhouettenocturne.com
www.paranormalromanceblog.com

SN61822

REQUEST YOUR FREE BOOKS!
2 FREE NOVELS PLUS 2
FREE GIFTS!

From the Heart, For the Heart

YES! Please send me 2 FREE Harlequin® Romance novels and my 2 FREE gifts (gifts are worth about $10). After receiving them, if I don't wish to receive any more books, I can return the shipping statement marked "cancel". If I don't cancel, I will receive 4 brand-new novels every month and be billed just $3.84 per book in the U.S. or $4.24 per book in Canada. That's a savings of at least 15% off the cover price! It's quite a bargain! Shipping and handling is just 50¢ per book.* I understand that accepting the 2 free books and gifts places me under no obligation to buy anything. I can always return a shipment and cancel at any time. Even if I never buy another book, the two free books and gifts are mine to keep forever.

114 HDN EYU3 314 HDN EYKG

Name   (PLEASE PRINT)

Address   Apt. #

City   State/Prov.   Zip/Postal Code

Signature (if under 18, a parent or guardian must sign)

Mail to the **Harlequin Reader Service:**
IN U.S.A.: P.O. Box 1867, Buffalo, NY 14240-1867
IN CANADA: P.O. Box 609, Fort Erie, Ontario L2A 5X3

Not valid to current subscribers of Harlequin Romance books.

**Are you a subscriber of Harlequin Romance books
and want to receive the larger-print edition?
Call 1-800-873-8635 today!**

* Terms and prices subject to change without notice. Prices do not include applicable taxes. Sales tax applicable in N.Y. Canadian residents will be charged applicable provincial taxes and GST. Offer not valid in Quebec. This offer is limited to one order per household. All orders subject to approval. Credit or debit balances in a customer's account(s) may be offset by any other outstanding balance owed by or to the customer. Please allow 4 to 6 weeks for delivery. Offer available while quantities last.

Your Privacy: Harlequin Books is committed to protecting your privacy. Our Privacy Policy is available online at www.eHarlequin.com or upon request from the Reader Service. From time to time we make our lists of customers available to reputable third parties who may have a product or service of interest to you. If you would prefer we not share your name and address, please check here. ☐

HR09R

Stay up-to-date on all your romance reading news!

The Harlequin Inside Romance newsletter is a **FREE** quarterly newsletter highlighting our upcoming series releases and promotions!

Go to eHarlequin.com/InsideRomance or e-mail us at InsideRomance@Harlequin.com to sign up to receive your FREE newsletter today!

IRN3PAQ209

HARLEQUIN® *Romance*®

Coming Next Month

Available November 10, 2009

For an early surprise this Christmas don't look under the
Christmas tree or in your stocking—look out for
Christmas Treats in your November Harlequin® Romance novels!

#4129 MONTANA, MISTLETOE, MARRIAGE
Christmas Treats
Patricia Thayer and Donna Alward
Join sisters Amelia and Kelley for Christmas on Rocking H Ranch as we
bring you two stories in one volume for double the romance!

#4130 THE MAGIC OF A FAMILY CHRISTMAS Susan Meier
Christmas Treats
All six-year-old Harry wants for Christmas is for his new mom, Wendy, to
marry so they can be a forever family. Will his wish come true?

#4131 CROWNED: THE PALACE NANNY Marion Lennox
Marrying His Majesty
When powerful prince Stefanos meets feisty nanny Elsa, sparks fly!
But will she ever agree to *Marrying His Majesty*? Find out in the final
installment of this majestic trilogy.

#4132 CHRISTMAS ANGEL FOR THE BILLIONAIRE Liz Fielding
Trading Places
Lady Rosanne Napier is *Trading Places* with a celebrity look-alike to
escape the spotlight and meets the man of her dreams in the start of
this brand-new duet.

#4133 COWBOY DADDY, JINGLE-BELL BABY Linda Goodnight
Christmas Treats
On a dusty Texas roadside, cowboy Dax delivers Jenna's baby. When he
offers her a job, neither expects her to become his housekeeper bride!

#4134 UNDER THE BOSS'S MISTLETOE Jessica Hart
Christmas Treats
Cassie was determined to ignore the attraction she felt for her new boss,
but that was before she was forced to pose under the mistletoe with
delectable Jake!

HRCNMBPA1009